Silent Tears
No More

Cedar River Daydreams (for girls 12–15):

#1 *New Girl in Town*
#2 *Trouble with a Capital "T"*
#3 *Jennifer's Secret*
#4 *Journey to Nowhere*
#5 *Broken Promises*
#6 *The Intruder*
#7 *Silent Tears No More*
#8 *Fill My Empty Heart*

Springflower Books (for girls 12–15):

Adrienne   *Melissa*
Erica   *Michelle*
Jill   *Paige*
Laina   *Sara*
Lisa   *Wendy*
Marty

Heartsong Books (for young adults):

Andrea   *Kara*
Anne   *Karen*
Carrie   *Leslie*
Colleen   *Rachel*
Cynthia   *Shelly*
Gillian   *Sherri*
Jenny   *Stacey*
Jocelyn   *Tiffany*

Silent Tears No More

Judy Baer

BETHANY HOUSE PUBLISHERS

MINNEAPOLIS, MINNESOTA 55438

A Division of Bethany Fellowship, Inc.

Silent Tears No More
Judy Baer

Library of Congress Catalog Card Number 89-082689

ISBN 1-55661-119-6

Published by Bethany House Publishers
A Ministry of Bethany Fellowship, Inc.
6820 Auto Club Road, Minneapolis, Minnesota 55438

Printed in the United States of America

For all my readers,
especially those who write to me
and brighten my day.

JUDY BAER received a B.A. in English and Education from Concordia College in Moorhead, Minnesota. She has had fifteen novels published and is a member of the National Romance Writers of America, the Society of Children's Book Writers and the National Federation of Press Women.

Two of her novels have been prizewinning bestsellers in the Bethany House SPRINGFLOWER SERIES (for girls 12–15); *Adrienne* and *Paige*. Both books have been awarded first place for juvenile fiction in the National Federation of Press Women's communications contest.

But Jesus said, "Let the children come to me, and do not hinder them; for to such belongs the kingdom of heaven."

Matthew 19:14

Chapter One

"I think he likes me, Lexi. I really think he does!" Binky McNaughton's pale eyes were shining and a huge smile laced her face. She flung herself against the well-worn chenille spread on her bed and clasped her hands over her head. "Can you believe it? Harry Cramer liking me?" Like a fish out of water, Binky flip-flopped from side to side across the bed.

Lexi Leighton grinned and tucked her feet beneath her as she sat cross-legged on a chair across from Binky. Her eyes traveled over the slightly shabby furniture that filled Binky's room. Everything in the McNaughton household was well used and worn, though immaculately clean. Sometimes Lexi took for granted the lovely things she had, but never when she came to visit her friend Binky.

Binky bolted upright on the bed and clapped her hands. "Harry and me! *Me?* Can you believe it?"

Lexi laughed out loud. She'd never seen Binky quite so overjoyed. Harry Cramer had smiled at Binky as they'd left school that afternoon. Binky acted as though Harry had given her the keys to a Rolls-Royce instead of a big grin and a conspiratorial wink, which seemed to hint that there could be something very special between them.

Binky had changed lately—in subtle ways. Binky

9

wasn't as skinny as she'd been. She looked less like a bean pole and more like a young woman. In fact, Binky looked downright attractive. Her eyes sparkled and her features were so animated that she virtually glowed. *Of course,* Lexi thought to herself, *Binky is in love.*

"He talked to me in study hall," Binky announced. "Three times. The last time I thought he was going to get into trouble." Binky's eyes glittered. "Over me. Can you believe it?"

"Of course I can believe it, dopey," Lexi said with a laugh. "Harry Cramer is interested in you. There's no getting around it."

"No one's ever been interested in me before," Binky protested disbelievingly. "What do you think's wrong with Harry that he'd want to be seen with me?"

"What's *wrong* with him?" Lexi protested. "The question is, what's wrong with everybody else that no one's been interested in you before now?"

Binky gave a highly unladylike snort. "I don't see why guys haven't been beating down my door for years. You think it has anything to do with the fact that I look like a skinny little stick figure?"

"But you look less like a stick figure all the time," Lexi grinned. "Harry's just the first to notice the . . . possibilities."

Binky convulsed into a fit of giggles. "He's so neat, Lexi. He really is. Tell me more about him."

"Well, I don't really know that much," Lexi began.

"But, he's a friend of Todd's," Binky pointed out. "And he is in the Emerald Tones. That means you know more about him than I do."

The Emerald Tones was Cedar River High School's pride and joy, a fine singing group that was building a reputation around the state.

"Well, Harry has a beautiful tenor voice," Lexi offered. "Mrs. Waverly has him do solos quite often."

"A singer. Isn't that romantic?" Binky gushed.

Lexi rolled her eyes. If she'd told Binky that Harry couldn't carry a note, Binky would have melted. If he spoke in a monotone, it would still delight Binky at this moment.

She clapped her hands. "Tell me more. I want to know all about him!"

Lexi held up her hand. "You're going to have to ask Todd these questions. I really don't know Harry that well. He hangs out with the guys in the Emerald Tones."

"Do you know anything about his family?" Binky asked eagerly. Sherlock Holmes on a big case couldn't have been more persistent.

"Well, Todd says he has two older brothers. Both in college. I know Harry's dad is an electrician because it was Cramer Electric that did the wiring on my dad's veterinary clinic. I think his mother is a nurse. Why don't you ask Harry?"

Binky's mouth puckered into a little round *O*. "Oh, I couldn't do that. I'd be too scared."

Lexi groaned. "Scared? Don't be crazy. You just start a conversation and—"

Binky waved her hands. She obviously didn't want to talk about starting any conversations with Harry. She wanted to get every detail of his life history settled in her mind.

"He's not in basketball, is he? Egg never mentioned that."

"Track, I think," Lexi said. "A runner." If she'd told Binky Harry was a trapeze artist, she would have been satisfied.

Binky settled herself again on the corner of the iron bed. "Well, I know he's smart. I read the honor roll every month and he's always right there at the top." She frowned. "I wish I'd paid a little more attention to his name when it came up in the *Cedar River Review*."

The *Cedar River Review* was the high school paper on which Lexi worked. "If I'd known he was going to like me, I would have been reading about him all the time," Binky said with convoluted logic.

"Well, no matter what else he does," Lexi concluded, "he's very nice. I like Harry. Todd says he's a great guy."

Binky smiled a dopey grin. "Nice. He's really nice." Then her eyes brightened. "And gorgeous too. I think his hair is naturally curly, don't you?"

Lexi threw her hands in the air and yelped. "I give up. I surrender. This is hopeless. I can't carry on a civilized conversation with you when all you want to talk about is Harry Cramer!"

Binky ignored her and continued dreamily. "His eyes are green, I think. Or maybe they're hazel. I've never really been close enough," she giggled. "I should have looked in study hall today, but I could see Mr. Raddis glaring at us out of the corner of his eye. I thought, *If we get into trouble, Harry might never talk to me again*—that would be terrible!" Binky rattled on like a rock in a tin can.

Lexi decided it was time to calm Binky down a bit by changing the subject. She cast her eyes around the room for a topic of conversation, and her gaze fell on a picture of the McNaughton family taken the Christmas before. Binky's brother was grinning from the photo.

Impulsively, Lexi asked, "What's the Egg doing, Binky? I haven't talked to him for a few days."

Egg, or Edward, McNaughton was Binky's older brother. He was a taller version of his sister—just as skinny, just as flighty and equally sweet.

Binky gave her a pained look. "Egg? Why do you want to know about him? Egg's been weird lately."

"Weird?" Lexi echoed.

"Weirder. Weirder than ever." Binky stubbed her toe into the carpet. "I think he's going off the deep end, Lexi. Maybe we'll have to put him in a home or something."

"Don't you think you're exaggerating *just a little*?" Lexi asked. Egg and Binky were famous for saying outrageous things about each other and fighting like cats and dogs. But, if someone else were to say a negative thing about one of them, the other would come to his defense in a flash.

"He's still eating all that goop, you know. All those health foods? He's lifting weights too. I can hear terrible groans coming from his weight room. You should see him in the morning, Lexi. He puts this stuff in the blender for breakfast." Binky shuddered. "It's wheat germ and brewer's yeast and Vitamin C powder and yogurt; and when Mom's not looking, I think he throws in a raw egg too—yuk! He's become a compulsive health nut. I think too much of it could make him sick."

Before Lexi had time to question the logic of Binky's statement, there was a rap on Binky's bedroom door.

"Anybody in here?" Egg poked his head around the partially open door and peered into the room. With no response from the girls, he entered. He was wearing a red mesh muscle shirt, long shorts in a splashy print of red, black, pink and yellow, old tennis shoes, and no socks. He was also just as skinny as ever, and Lexi wondered if the new health regime was doing Egg any good.

He didn't look a single bit more muscular or healthy than he had when she'd first met him. In fact, she couldn't tell that he'd been lifting weights at all.

"What are you two doing in here?" Egg grinned knowingly as he ambled into the center of the room. Then he put his forearm to his mouth and began to make kissing sounds. His eyes were twinkling. "My sister has a *crush* on Harry Cramer. Oooh—ooh." He rolled his eyes and continued the disgusting noises.

"Shut your mouth, Edward McNaughton, or I'm gonna shut it for you!" Binky screeched as she reached for a pillow on her bed. It went flying and hit Egg in the face, just as he opened his mouth.

"You little twirp. Just for that, I'm not gonna tell you what Harry Cramer said about you in study hall."

Binky froze as she was about to fling another pillow. "Harry Cramer talked about me?"

"Yeah," Egg said, mustering as much dignity as he could with feathers from the down pillow stuck in his hair. "And now you'll never know what he had to say. You'll go to your grave still wondering." Egg turned around and Binky lunged forward, grabbing him by the waistband of his shorts.

"Hey! Let go."

"Not until you tell me what Harry Cramer said, Egg McNaughton."

"Let go of my shorts. You're gonna pull 'em off."

"I'd be doing you a favor. They're ugly anyway. You get back in here and tell me what Harry Cramer said about me."

"No! You threw a pillow at me. And quit insulting my shorts."

"Ooooohweeee!" Binky screeched. "Quit teasing me, Egg. Tell me. *Please,* tell me."

Lexi decided it was time for her to step in. "All right, you two. Break it up."

"She started it," Egg muttered.

Binky made a face. Then she apologized. "I'm sorry, Egg, if I insulted you in any way. Now, what did Harry Cramer say about me?"

Egg gave a resigned little sigh, knowing there was really no way out of finishing this conversation with his sister. "He asked about you, that's all."

"*Asked* about me? Asked about *me*? What does that mean? What did he say? What were his words *exactly*?"

Egg rolled his eyes, and Lexi covered her mouth so Binky wouldn't catch her smile.

"He asked about you, that's all. He said, 'Egg, my man, where's that kid sister of yours?' "

"He called me your '*kid* sister'?" Binky wailed, her voice heavy with disappointment.

"Well, maybe he didn't say it exactly that way."

Binky gave a screech and lunged for Egg. "You're teasing me again. Quit lying to me. Don't you do that again, you hear?"

This time, Egg raised his hands in submission. "All right. All right. Harry said, 'How's your sister doing, Egg?' And I said, 'Fine, I guess.' And he said, 'What's she doing after school these days?'"

"What did you tell him?" Binky pleaded.

"I don't know what you do after school. I guess I told him that you and Lexi usually hang out together. Nothing special. I told him you didn't have a job or anything."

"Ooooh." Now Binky's eyes were glittering. "He wanted to know where I went after school."

Egg rolled his eyes. "I should have told him that we were committing you to a mental institution," he said bluntly.

Binky ignored the snide comment. "Thanks, Egg. I'll see you later."

Egg, more than happy to leave, saluted Lexi and retreated from the room.

Binky floated to the edge of her bed. She perched there, her hands on her knees, her eyes staring dreamily out the window toward the yard. "He really must like me, Lexi. He never would have asked Egg about me if he didn't."

"Of course he does," Lexi said. "What else have we been talking about around here?"

Binky gave a sigh. "I just can't believe it, that's all. I've never had a boyfriend before. I've never known anyone who liked me."

"I like you," Lexi told her. "And Todd. Ben's crazy about you and—"

Binky stood up and studied herself in the mirror. "Frankly, I never imagined any guy would ever be interested in me."

"Well, that's ridiculous," Lexi said. "What gave you an idea like that?"

"I'm so skinny. I'm not pretty like you." Binky looked gloomy. "I don't know. I just thought guys had better taste than that."

Yelping her protest at Binky's put-down, Lexi picked up the pillow that Egg had left on the floor and threw it at her. "What you need is a bit of self-confidence, Binky McNaughton. Too bad they don't sell it. I'd buy you a bottle. Then you could go up to Harry Cramer tomorrow and say—"

Binky uttered a little gasp. "Tomorrow!" She jumped to her feet, ran to her closet and threw open the doors. Lexi could see a neat but sparse row of blouses and skirts.

"I have to figure out what I'm going to wear tomorrow," Binky announced. "When I see Harry I have to look my best."

Lexi blinked twice. Was it possible? Binky actually caring about what she wore?

"Oh, oh," Lexi said. "A spaceship must have landed and picked up my friend Bonita McNaughton and left *you* in her place. It's got to be. The Binky I know would never care about what she wore."

Binky shot her a disgusted look. "That was the *old* Binky McNaughton." She did a pirouette in the doorway of the closet. "This is the *new* Bonita McNaughton. Because of Harry Cramer, *she* cares very much what she looks like."

"Still," Lexi said as she smiled and stretched, "I

don't think you have to worry too much about what you wear. Harry likes you the way you are, and you haven't been thinking about it at all. Anyway, you want a guy who cares about what's on the inside, not the outside."

"Easy for you to talk," Binky moaned.

"Why do you say that?" Lexi wondered.

"Because you have Todd."

"Todd?" Lexi echoed. "What does he have to do with all of this?"

"You've already got a boyfriend. A great one. A handsome one. One that any girl in school would give her eyeteeth to have. This is the first time any guy has shown any interest in me. I can't do anything that might mess it up."

"I think you've got it a little mixed up already, Binky," Lexi said softly. "It's not like Todd and I are just boyfriend and girlfriend, we're—" Lexi struggled for the right words. "We're *life* friends."

It was true, Lexi thought, as she considered what she'd said. She and Todd *were* life friends, best friends. Their friendship didn't depend upon the fact that they were of the opposite sex. Instead, it was a friendship of two kindred spirits. They had a wonderful time together and liked to spend most of their free time in shared activities. There was a unique understanding between them—each giving the other space alone as well. Anyway, Lexi's parents didn't approve of early dating or going steady. They understood that she and Todd shared a friendship that went far beyond anything as superficial as a fleeting boy/girl relationship.

While Lexi was thinking about Todd, Binky was

staring into her closet with a frown. "I can't believe how few clothes I have to wear," she said.

Lexi peeked over Binky's shoulders into the closet and nodded. "It is pretty sparse."

"Seems like whenever I get any money, there are just so many other things I'd rather buy than clothes," Binky said forlornly. "But now, when I see this—"

Still gazing into the almost empty closet, her shoulders suddenly straightened and she snapped her fingers. "I know. I'll just have to buy some new ones!"

Lexi stared at Binky doubtfully. "Buy new ones? With what? Aren't you the person who's broke every minute of every day?"

"Then I'll have to get some money," Binky said matter-of-factly. "And I know just how to do it." With that surprising statement, she dashed for her bedroom door.

Within a few seconds, Binky was back with the morning paper.

"There are jobs in the want ads. Tons of them. All listed in neat little rows. All I have to do is pick one out and go apply."

"Just like that?" Lexi said with disbelief. "You expect anyone who is advertising in the paper for help to hire a teenage girl who just walks in from the street?"

Binky hesitated for only a moment. "Sure. Why not? I'm a good worker."

"But they don't know that, Binky. You don't have any job experience."

Binky's lips turned into a pout. "I can't get a job

'cause I don't have any experience and I can't get experience because I don't have a job. So where does that leave me?"

"Doing something as I do?" Lexi said hopefully. "Like working for my father?"

"Fat chance," Binky muttered. "Not for me. But there must be some way for teenagers to get work."

Binky opened the paper to the "help wanted" section and began to read. " 'Needed immediately, dietitian. Four-year degree, experience necessary.' Nope. 'Wanted. Part-time help in filling station, pumping gas. Must be able to do minor repairs.' " She wrinkled her nose. "Ick. I hate getting grease on my fingers. 'Nurse, piano tuner, engineer, electrician, teacher,' " Binky snorted. "They all want people who are old. Nobody wants a young person like me . . . How about a waitress? I could be a waitress!" Binky said emphatically.

Lexi bit her tongue. She didn't want to point out that clumsiness was one of Binky's strong traits. She could just imagine the girl serving a tray full of soup tureens and having them all land on the customers' heads.

Binky thought about it for a moment herself and then shook her head. "No, I guess that won't do. I'd hate to spill something."

Then she tore the want ads in half and tossed a portion toward Lexi. "Here, Lexi, start reading and don't quit until you find something I can apply for. After all, now that Harry is in my life, I really do need a job."

Chapter Two

"It's a lot harder than I thought, Lexi," Binky groaned. "I never dreamed that finding a job would be this difficult." She was curled forlornly in one corner of the couch in the Leighton living room. Her shoulders sagged and she wore a gloomy expression.

"You've just got to keep at it, Binky," Lexi encouraged. "Don't give up now. I'm sure the right job is out there just waiting for you."

Binky gave one of her unladylike snorts. "Right. But where is it waiting? Siberia? It certainly doesn't seem to be waiting for me here in Cedar River!"

"Are you sure you're not just giving up too soon?" Lexi wondered.

"Too soon?" Binky echoed. She stretched out her slim legs along the length of the couch and slid into a prone position with her head dangling over the edge. "Do you realize the number of places I've gone for interviews? I've been to practically every store in the mall. I've applied at every cafe within the city limits and I've called every single business that advertises in the newspaper. Do you realize how many stores *don't* want a sixteen-year-old to work for them?"

"Don't take it personally, Binky."

"No, maybe not. But everybody does seem to have all the help they need. There are even jobs in this town that are handed down from generation to generation."

Lexi looked at her friend blankly. "What do you mean?"

"I've talked to people who got their job from their big brother who got it from his older sister. When you're about to graduate, you put in a good word for the next youngest in your family."

Lexi chuckled. "That might be fine for some people, Binky, but would you really want to take over any job Egg had started?"

A smile crept across Binky's delicate features. "True, true. I wouldn't want to be connected in any way with anything Egg had his paws into. It's bad enough having the same last name." Binky snapped her fingers. "*That's* probably why I'm not getting a job. They've already heard of Egg McNaughton and don't want anything to do with a relative of his!"

By this time, both girls were laughing and Binky's outlook had cheered considerably.

"There's still got to be a job out there," Lexi said. "Todd told me last night that Harry Cramer just got a position as a bus boy in that fancy new restaurant opening over on 28th Avenue."

"The Willows?" Binky smiled widely now. "Harry told me. In fact," and her expression turned blissful, "he asked me if I'd like to go there sometime."

"Really?" Lexi was impressed. "He asked you out on a date?"

Binky shrugged her shoulders. "Not exactly. He said he wanted to show me the place where he was working and give me an opportunity to try the food. Does that sound like a real date to you?"

Lexi looked at her friend in amazement. She hadn't realized just how insecure Binky felt about her newly budding relationship with Harry. "Well, I suppose it depends on if he sits down and eats with you or just buses your dishes when you're done."

Binky grinned. "Yeah, maybe it *is* a real date. Wouldn't that be great? Harry is sooooo nice. He talks to me just like I'm a real human being."

"Well, you *are* a real human being," Lexi chided as she busied herself picking out all the black jelly beans from the dish on the coffee table. "Have you forgotten that?"

"It's easy to," Binky grimaced, "after all, with Egg for a brother, you sometimes forget what species the entire family is from."

Lexi, accustomed to the way Binky and Egg talked about each other, ignored the jibe. Just then, Edward McNaughton came meandering through the living room. In his hand was a slightly misshapen whole wheat bun filled with something pale and quivery—very unlike any meat Lexi had seen before. There were little hair-like green sprouts dangling from the edges of the sandwich, and something yellow oozing onto Egg's hand.

"What is that, Egg?" Lexi asked. "Should you be eating it?"

Egg glanced down at the sandwich in his hand. "It's a tofu burger with sprouts and mustard. Do you want one?"

"Blech! Double blech!" Binky sat on the far side of the room, making grotesque, gagging noises and clutching her stomach. "Where did you come from, anyway, Egg?"

Egg's eyes flashed as he turned to her. "Lexi's mom let me in the back door. I just wondered what you guys were up to. And you can knock it off, Binky, about my food. It's not funny. This stuff is good for you. Anyway, why should I listen to an unhealthy little pip-squeak like you?"

"Takes a pip to know the squeak," Binky shot back. "You're going to kill yourself eating that stuff. I've seen goop in mom's compost heap that looks more appetizing than that."

"Tofu is high protein. I eat it for strength."

"Looks like something that comes out of your nose when you have a cold," Binky countered graphically.

"You quit it, Bonita McNaughton! You're being rude and stupid. You don't know anything about this."

Lexi was startled to hear the anger in Egg's voice. He and Binky were accustomed to teasing and tormenting each other. She was surprised that Egg had paid any attention at all.

"You don't have to get so hot under the collar," Binky retorted.

"And you don't have to criticize my eating habits," Egg shot back.

"Well, excuuuuuuse me," Binky said, miffed.

Lexi, hearing the exchange, was surprised to realize how important it was to Egg to build himself up. Otherwise, he never would have defended the awful-looking sandwich.

Binky gathered herself together and stood up with as much dignity as she could muster. "Let's get out of here. That sandwich is polluting the air."

Lexi could see Egg stifle a retort and stuff the rest of the sandwich into his mouth. As he did so, a little glob of mustard dripped on his chin.

"Goodbye and good riddance," he mumbled. "Not to you, Lexi," he amended.

Lexi took Binky by the arm and steered her toward the front door. "Why don't we check the job board at the employment office, Binky? Maybe there will be something new posted. See you later, Egg."

That suggestion turned Binky's attention away from Egg, who glowered at her as they escaped through the front door.

Lexi gave a little sigh of relief when they reached the bottom of the steps. Egg was certainly touchy. Maybe that weird food he was eating *was* making him sick.

"You see what I mean, don't you?" Binky said with a frown. "Egg's so grumpy lately. He's always stuffing himself full of that horrible glop. Mom had fried eggs and caramel rolls for breakfast today, and Egg went to the counter and mixed up something in the blender that looked as if it belonged in the sewer."

"Well," Lexi replied mildly, "just because you don't approve of his eating habits doesn't mean you should be so hard on him."

Binky looked guilty. "Yeah, I suppose I have been. If he can stand to put it in his mouth—"

"And no matter how it looks, tofu *is* a very healthy food."

"I suppose," Binky agreed doubtfully. "Maybe I'll just leave Egg alone. I think it's a stage. He'll outgrow it, right?"

Lexi wasn't so sure, but she nodded hopefully. She'd had a friend back in Grover's Point, where she'd lived before, who was a health nut like Egg. The last she'd heard, that girl was a vegetarian, refusing to eat anything that wasn't organically grown. With all the stuff that had been in the newspaper about pesticides and chemicals and fertilizer, maybe Egg was on the right track. Still, it would be hard to give up a burger and fries for tofu with sprouts and mustard.

————————

They were halfway to the employment office when Binky and Lexi saw Anna Marie Arnold stepping out of a dress shop. The girl turned to look longingly back toward the window.

"Hi, Anna Marie," Binky greeted her as Lexi waved and smiled. "Shopping?"

Anna Marie, a shy, heavy-set girl from their class, was someone Lexi hadn't learned to know very well. Anna Marie was pretty, with soft brown curls and pale blue eyes that made her look dreamy and unapproachable. As they neared, they noticed how Anna Marie self-consciously tugged at the front of her jacket.

Perhaps one of the reasons she'd never gotten to know Anna Marie, Lexi mused, was that she had a tendency to keep people at a distance. She was obviously self-conscious about her size and weight.

A feeling of sympathy swept over Lexi. Anna was

obviously pleased to see them, yet at the same time, nervously clinging to the front of her over-sized jacket as if to hide herself.

More than once at school, Lexi had overheard members of the Hi-Five making snide remarks directly to Anna about her size. Minda had even tried to use Anna as an example of how *not* to dress in her fashion column. Thankfully, Mrs. Drummond had caught the barb and deleted it from the column.

Her nickname, Banana Anna, came from her passion for banana splits at the Hamburger Shack. Lexi hadn't seen Anna for a while. Unfortunately, she seemed larger than ever.

"Did you find anything?" Binky wondered, tipping her head toward the dress shop. "Anything really cute?"

Anna shook her head. "No. Nothing for me. There were lots of things in there that *you* might like, though."

Binky wrinkled her nose. "Not unless they are giving away things free. Lexi and I are on our way to the employment office to read the job board. I'm broke, Anna."

"Well, good luck. I hope you find something." Anna smiled at them.

When Anna had turned the corner and disappeared from sight, Binky gave a low whistle through her teeth. "Poor kid. She must have a terrible time finding clothes."

Lexi nodded in agreement. "She certainly doesn't smile much. At least not at school."

"Who could?" Binky shot back. "Especially considering the way the Hi-Five's treat her. Sometimes

I wonder what those girls use for brains. Anna can't help how she is. She's pretty, she's smart and she's nice. What does it matter if she's overweight, anyway? Last year I had a locker next to her and do you know what some kids did? They went to the day-old bread place and bought about a hundred loaves of bread and stuffed them into Anna's locker with a note saying, 'Here's a little snack in case you didn't get enough for lunch.' When she opened her locker, all the stale, squashed bread fell out at her feet."

"How awful!" Lexi gasped.

Binky nodded sadly. "It was terrible. I was standing there switching my books when it happened. I thought I was going to die, just looking at the expression on Anna's face. But do you know what she did?"

Lexi shook her head, suddenly furious at the unkind trick.

"She turned to the crowd that had gathered behind her and just shrugged her shoulders calmly and said, 'You can tell that the guys who did this weren't very smart. There's not a single jar of peanut butter in here.'"

"That's great!" Lexi chortled.

"Yeah, it was pretty spectacular. Everybody who'd been standing there horrified started to laugh and help her clean up the mess. Everybody was joking. I remember Todd came up and put his arm around her, gave her a squeeze and said, 'Good comeback, Anna. You showed them.'"

"Sounds like Todd," Lexi said with a smile.

"Anyway, the trick didn't work like they'd intended, but I thought that for weeks afterward Anna looked even sadder than before. She was cautious opening her locker from then on."

Before Lexi could comment, she realized that they were at the employment office. Binky walked to the job board and began to read aloud from the list of ads pinned to the corkboard.

"I could work at a car wash," she quipped, "or as a fry cook at a greasy spoon. There sure isn't much to choose from. Every good job in Cedar River must be taken."

"How about this one?" Lexi pointed to a small hand-printed ad near the bottom of the bulletin board. "This looks new."

"Hmmmm." Binky studied the slip of paper intently. "Young family seeking part-time babysitter/ nanny for child, age nine. Looking for a responsible girl who is good with children." Binky looked hopeful. "Well, I'm certainly responsible enough and I'm excellent with children." Then her eyes twinkled. "Of all ages. Not just anyone could deal with my brother Egg!"

"Copy that one down," Lexi ordered. "It just might be the job for you."

"Lexi, do you really think I'd be a good babysitter/ nanny? What if I didn't like the kid? What if—"

"Well, there's no way you'll ever know unless you check it out," Lexi pointed out logically.

"Right." Binky scribbled down the telephone number on the scrap of paper she'd carried in her pocket. "I'll do it first thing tomorrow. Right now, I'm starving. Do you have time to stop at the Hamburger Shack for something to eat?"

"Of course. Watching Egg eat that tofu burger made me very hungry—for some real food, that is."

"Well, I know I'm not ordering anything that looks like green and yellow pus!" Binky retorted. "I want a double cheeseburger, an order of fries, a double chocolate malt and a. . . ."

She was still rattling off the list of food she wanted when they walked through the door of the Hamburger Shack. Suddenly she became very quiet. Binky stood stock-still in the doorway.

"Now, what's wrong?" Lexi asked as she stepped on the heels of Binky's tennis shoes and nearly knocked her to the floor.

"Look. Look in that corner."

Lexi glanced around. There weren't many people in the Hamburger Shack. Most of them were strangers. The only ones she knew were at the back—Todd Winston and Harry Cramer.

"Oh. I see what you mean," Lexi said with a smile.

"It's him. It's Harry and he's here with Todd."

"Well, let's go say hi to them," Lexi suggested.

"I can't. I can't. I'll just die."

"Well, I'm certainly not going to stand here in the doorway acting like one half of a comedy team. *I'll* go talk to Todd and Harry."

With a pitiful moan of delight and fear, Binky followed.

"Hi, guys," Lexi greeted Todd and Harry cheerfully as she slid into the booth beside Todd, leaving the space next to Harry for Binky.

"Hi yourself. What's up?"

"We've just been to the employment office. Binky's looking for work."

"Still no luck finding anything?" Harry turned to Binky with a look of genuine concern in his eyes.

"Uh, uh, uh . . . one lead," Binky finally blurted. "A babysitter/nanny type position."

"That might be all right," Harry said with a nod. "Especially if you're good with kids."

Lexi watched and listened to the conversation between the two of them. Binky hung on Harry's every word as though he were giving a State of the Union address rather than just small talk. But Harry didn't seem to mind. In fact, he appeared flattered by Binky's devoted attention.

Lexi felt Todd kick her beneath the table. He leaned over and whispered into her ear, "Are you seeing what I'm seeing? Is that Binky McNaughton flirting?"

It was true. Binky *was* flirting. She was batting her stubby little eyelashes a mile a minute and smiling coyly at Harry.

Now she'd seen everything, Lexi thought to herself. Binky McNaughton—tomboy—falling in love.

Todd pointed to a sign on the window of the Hamburger Shack. "Did you see that?"

"The poster about the circus?" Lexi asked. "I read it yesterday when I went by. It's coming soon, isn't it?"

"It starts tomorrow. Harry and I were just talking about it."

"Do you like circuses?" Lexi asked, turning to Harry.

"Sure. I enjoy the lion tamer, especially."

"I love circuses," Lexi said with enthusiasm. "Grover's Point was too small to have a circus come to town. We always had to travel somewhere to see one. Some of my best memories are from the circuses we've seen."

"Me too," Binky chimed in, determined not to be left out of the conversation. "I like the high-wire acts, trapeze artists and all those balancing stunts. The higher the better."

"Without a net?" Todd finished.

"Definitely," Binky returned with relish. "What's the thrill if you know they'll be caught if they fall?"

"Bloodthirsty, aren't you?" Todd said with a chuckle. "The trapeze artist on the poster doesn't have a net beneath him. Maybe we should take you, Binky. You could have lots of fun waiting to see if he's going to tumble."

"And I like it when there are acts in all three rings at once so you have to keep turning your head and never get to see one whole act. And when thirty clowns come pouring out of that little Volkswagen . . . and I like the cotton candy and—"

"She definitely likes the circus." Todd turned to Lexi. "How about it, Lex? Should we all go tomorrow night?"

Lexi glanced from Binky to Harry and then back to Todd. "Well, I suppose I could. I know my parents wouldn't mind."

"Binky? How about you?" Todd stared across the table.

"Me? I, well, I suppose so. It isn't too expensive, is it?"

"Don't worry about the expense," Harry interrupted. "It'll be my treat, Binky. I'll take you."

At that moment, Lexi wished for a camera to record the expression on Binky's face. Shock, surprise, delight. Here it was. An invitation to her first *real* date!

The subject of the circus occupied most of the conversation while they ate. Binky didn't seem nearly as hungry as she had indicated earlier before entering the Hamburger Shack. In fact, she ate only a few bites of her cheeseburger and left most of her fries untouched.

After saying goodbye to Todd and Harry, Binky and Lexi turned the opposite direction and walked toward home. Lexi, at least, walked home. Binky, navigated a few inches above the ground on some sort of a dreamy, floating cloud. Under her breath she muttered, "A circus. A real date. Not just an accidental date or 'I'm-doing-this-to-be-nice-to-you' date, but a real one. Isn't that right, Lexi?"

"It's real. Real as they come," Lexi agreed with a smile. "Todd and I were there to vouch for you."

"You take all this for granted because you have Todd," Binky pointed out, "but for me, well, this is special!"

Indeed it was. Binky was so inflated with joy she reminded Lexi of a helium balloon. More than once on the walk home, Lexi wished she had some sort of string to pull her friend back to earth, but Binky was determined to stay in orbit where Harry Cramer had sent her.

Chapter Three

"Lexi! Guess what? Lexi? Are you awake?" Binky's excited voice came bubbling across the telephone line.

Lexi scrubbed at her eyes with the back of her hand. "I am now," she mumbled, her mouth still cottony with sleep. "What time is it?"

"It's nine fifteen. I thought you always got up early."

"On Saturdays?" Lexi muttered. "Not if I can help it. What's going on?"

"Job Service just called. I talked to them about that nanny position we copied down yesterday and they've lined me up for an interview. It's perfect for me, Lexi. Absolutely perfect. The family needs a sitter from four to ten P.M. some weeknights and all day Saturdays. The schedule varies though, so I'll have plenty of time off. The family is opening a new restaurant, and sometimes their daughter can be with them."

"Sounds perfect," Lexi said sleepily. "But you

sound awfully excited. There must be something else."

"You know me too well," Binky grumbled. "I can't keep anything from you. The new restaurant these people are opening? Well, it's the one Harry's working at!"

"Uh-huh," Lexi replied craftily. "So you and Harry will have the same employer."

"Isn't it incredible? One more thing that we'll have in common."

As if they needed another, Lexi thought to herself. Binky and Harry were already so charmed with each other that they hardly needed another thing in common to solidify their relationship.

"The husband and wife are both chefs," Binky explained. "So they both need to be there for the rush hours. They're anticipating the hours between four and ten will be their busiest. I'm supposed to stay flexible until they know exactly when they'll need me."

"What about things you have to do after school, Binky? Schoolwork or chores or—"

"No problem. They have only the one child—a nine-year-old girl. She can come with me if I have to run errands and we can do our homework together."

"Sounds as if you've got it all planned out."

Binky's delighted laughter danced over the line. "Well, it really sounds like an easy job. Plus, the pay is good, and it's another link to Harry. What more could I ask for?"

"Nothing, I guess," Lexi said as she stretched sleepily. "Actually, all *I* need now is a chance to go back to sleep."

"Oh, but you can't," Binky said emphatically.

"I can't? Why not?"

"Because I need you. You have to come with me for the interview."

"Oh, I don't think I should, Binky. Besides, the way you were talking, I thought you practically had the job wrapped up."

"Oh, I'm sure I will have," Binky said. "But I *do* have the interview, and I really need you to come along, Lexi—for moral support."

"I don't know, Binky."

"Please? Listen, Lexi. You're my best friend in the whole world. This is really scary. I've never done anything like this before. Besides, I want this job so badly, I don't want to do anything that might blow it for me. You're so poised and confident, and you can tell me exactly what I need to do and say. And I have to be there at ten o'clock! You *have* to come with me."

"I really don't think it's going to impress anyone if you need *me* along for moral support!" Lexi pointed out.

"But the interview is at The Willows. They don't even have to know you're there. Just come along for me. You can sit in the lobby. There's probably a telephone there. You could pretend to make a phone call."

"Gee, thanks," Lexi muttered.

Binky's voice lowered to a desperate pleading. "I'm going to need your prayers on this one, Lexi. I'm really scared."

At that, Lexi finally broke down. "Oh, all right. I suppose I can stand in the entryway and pretend I'm a potted plant while you're doing your thing."

"Thanks, Lexi. You don't know how much this means to me. You're the best friend and moral support any girl could have!" Binky squealed. "Ooh! Look at the time. Gotta go. I'll be over to pick you up in a few minutes."

Lexi blinked at the click as Binky hung up the phone. She'd barely returned the receiver to its cradle when it rang again. It was Binky. This time her voice was panicky.

"They just called me back, Lexi—the people at Job Service. They're moving my interview to this afternoon."

"Good," Lexi said. "Now I can go back to sleep."

"No, you can't!" Binky's voice reached a high-pitched wail. "There's too much to do!"

"But I thought you just said the interview was going to be this afternoon?"

"It is. It just gives me more time to think about what I'm going to wear to the interview."

"Oh, for crying out loud," Lexi groaned. "Binky, just wear something nice."

"But don't you see? That's the problem. I don't have anything nice. That's why I need the job. And Friday is the circus. I don't have any money to buy anything for the interview or the circus. If I don't have the job, I'll never have any money. What can I do?"

It was apparent to Lexi that she was not going to get back to sleep this morning. "Why don't I come over and help you figure out your wardrobe?" Lexi volunteered.

"Would you?" Binky's voice sounded hopeful again. "You can make an outfit out of practically nothing. If we can pull something together for the interview *and* for the circus, by this time next week, I'll have a paycheck. Then you and I can go shopping!"

"Sounds fine to me," Lexi said, "But let's make that shopping trip after eleven o'clock next Saturday!"

"Come soon?" Binky pleaded.

"Right away," Lexi assured her friend. "Soon as I get dressed. Bye."

Lexi pulled a brush through her hair and ate a piece of toast as she finished buttoning her blouse. She was ready to leave the house when the doorbell rang.

"Busy morning," Lexi's mom remarked with a smile. "And I thought you were planning to sleep in."

Lexi rolled her eyes. "Next time, I'm going to announce it to all my friends instead of just to my family."

"Hi, sleepy head, still eating breakfast?" Lexi's friend Jennifer Golden appeared in the doorway of the kitchen.

"Trying to. I'm supposed to be on an emergency mission to rescue Binky from the perils of her closet."

"Oh yeah? And how are you supposed to do that?"

"She's got a job interview this afternoon, and a date with Harry Cramer on Friday for the circus. She's panicking because she has nothing to wear. I told her I'd come over to see if we could put something together that would make her feel like a knock-out. Want to come along?"

Jennifer grinned. "Sure. You know I'm great at telling other people what to do. I'm just lousy at taking advice."

The door flew open as the two girls arrived at the McNaughton household. "There you are—Hi, Jennifer. Come on in," Binky said without prelude. "I've been looking through my closet and it's absolutely barren. I might have to go naked tonight."

"Do you think she's being slightly over-dramatic?" Jennifer asked as she turned to Lexi. "Is this truly a person in crisis?"

Lexi was about to retort when a horrible crunching sound came from somewhere in the house.

"Eeeauggghhh!"

"What was *that*?" Jennifer's eyes widened. "Sounds like someone being murdered in your basement."

Binky fluttered her hand in the air. "Oh, never mind that. It's just Egg."

"Egg is being murdered in the basement?" Jennifer persisted.

"No, he's lifting weights."

"Eeeauggghhh!"

"Does he always sound like that?" Jennifer wondered.

"Sometimes it's worse," Binky said in disgust. "Every time he adds pounds to the weights, the noises get louder."

Between the groaning sounds, Lexi could hear heavy breathing and the clanking of metal.

Binky turned to her and shrugged. "I told you, Lexi, he's going crazy. He eats something that looks like a hockey puck, and then he lies there in the basement grunting and groaning and straining. Then he comes up and makes another concoction in the blender that looks like pig slop. He's simply going crazy."

By this time, Binky was pacing the floor—alternately waving her hands and running her fingers through her hair.

"Love your hairdo," Jennifer said sarcastically. "Who did it for you? A passing tornado?"

Binky paused long enough to look in the mirror. Wisps of hair stuck out everywhere as though she'd stuck a finger in a light socket and electrified her scalp. She groaned and plopped her hands on top of her head. "How can I get a job if I look like a freak?" she screeched to no one in particular. "No wardrobe, no hairdo. I'll never get this job and Harry will never ask me out again and I'm going to be a poverty stricken old maid. It's the end of my life."

"Eeeauggghhh!"

"And my brother's going to be committed to an insane asylum. Life as I know it is over, over, over!"

Jennifer and Lexi exchanged glances. "You can cut the drama, Binky," Jennifer suggested.

"Yeah," Lexi added. "We've come to save your day, remember?"

Binky stared at them morosely. "Too late. It's already ruined."

Lexi took Binky by the elbow and steered her up the stairs. "Let's go to your room so I can see what you've got in your closet. While I'm doing that, Jennifer can fix your hair."

Binky looked doubtfully at Jennifer as they mounted the stairs. "Aren't you the one who shaved parts of your head?"

"I was in a slightly rebellious stage then," Jennifer said with a grin. "Come on. I promise to behave." She steered Binky toward a chair and pushed her down. In one quick movement, she picked up a brush and began to smooth Binky's hair into a side pony tail.

While Jennifer was working, Lexi opened the door to Binky's closet. "You'll never find anything in there, Lexi. I can't believe all the junk I've accumulated. Nothing matches at all. Everything is either old or ragged or doesn't fit right. I just can't —"

Lexi ignored Binky's fussing as she sifted through the closet. After a few moments, she pulled out a bright print skirt with a soft fabric belt.

"Yuk!" Binky complained. "I hate that skirt."

"Why? I think it's beautiful fabric," Lexi said. "And it's cut so full. Look how it swirls." She spun the hanger around in the air.

"I think it's dumpy," Binky complained. "My mom made me buy it because she liked it."

"A-hah," Lexi nodded knowingly. "Now I understand why you don't like the skirt. Haven't you been thinking about different ways to wear it?"

"How many ways can you wear a skirt?" Binky wondered sourly. "Mom bought me an ivory blouse to go with it. It's in there somewhere."

Lexi shook her head. "Too plain. We need something more colorful." She studied the vivid red, pink, and green in the print. "How about this?" With a flourish, Lexi pulled a hot pink T-shirt out of the back of Binky's closet. It was sleeveless, and quite stylish with its scooped back criss-crossed with two small straps.

"I wear that with shorts!" Binky moaned.

43

Lexi nodded. "And now you'll wear it with this skirt."

With another swift movement, Lexi pulled the soft fabric belt off the skirt and handed it to Jennifer, who immediately tied it around the pony tail in Binky's hair. While she was doing that, Lexi took a wide black belt from another skirt and paired it with the bright skirt and T-shirt that she'd laid on display across the bed.

Binky remained doubtful as she dressed, but all her anxiety faded away when she saw herself in the mirror. The off-centered pony tail had lifted her hair away from her face and made her eyes the focal point of her pixy-like features. The skirt was bright and swirling around her legs, and the little pink shirt looked as though it had been purchased to go with the skirt.

"You look great, Binky," Jennifer announced with satisfaction.

"Great!" Binky retorted. "I look absolutely fabulous! You guys are miracle workers!" She spun happily in front of the mirror. "Listen, thanks so much. I haven't been feeling very good about myself lately. And you've both really helped."

Impulsively, Lexi gave her friend a hug. "You mustn't get so down on yourself, Binky," Lexi said softly. "You're great exactly the way you are. It doesn't matter how you're dressed or how much money you have . . ."

Binky gave a weak smile. "I know. I know. God loves me all the same and that's what counts."

Lexi nodded, glad the message she'd given Binky more than once was having some effect.

"Well, I hate to break this up," Jennifer said bluntly, "but if you guys are going to be at that interview, you don't have too much time."

Binky glanced frantically at the clock. "We should be leaving."

Jennifer waved her hand in a mock salute. "I'm going to the basement to see if Egg's still alive down there. Be sure to call me and let me know what happens with the interview."

The threesome trooped down the stairs together. Jennifer disappeared into the basement where the strange groaning sounds continued, while Binky and Lexi hurried out the front door and into the sunlight.

Chapter Four

As Binky and Lexi approached The Willows restaurant, Binky's confidence began to deteriorate.

The Willows was situated on Cumberland Road, a short, curved street on which several of Cedar River's finest shops and restaurants were located. Lexi remembered her parents had come to Cumberland Road for dinner on the evening of their eighteenth wedding anniversary.

Binky, on the other hand, couldn't remember any of her family coming to Cumberland Road for any reason other than to gawk at the beautiful displays in the shop windows.

"I can't do this, Lexi. I just can't do it."

"What do you mean? We're almost there. A few more steps to the right and—"

"You know what I mean. Look at this place." Binky waved a hand at the brightly covered awnings that shaded store windows and the sculptured pots filled with bright flowers marking various doorways. "If they own a business on this street, it means they're really elite people. You know what kind of family I'm from—we don't have a lot of money. And looking at Egg would tell you we don't have a lot of social graces. What do I think I'm doing here? I can't work for these people. Whatever made me think that they'd even consider hiring me?"

Lexi put her hand on Binky's forearm in a soothing gesture. "You're nervous, that's all. You're trying to convince yourself that you can't go for the interview. That's silly."

"They won't hire me," Binky muttered. "They'll take one look at me and know that I can't do the job. Why would they allow *me* to take care of their daughter when they work in a fancy place like this?"

"Fancy or rich doesn't necessarily mean better, you know," Lexi said softly.

"That's easy for you to say, Lexi," Binky retorted. "You're dad's a veterinarian and your mom's an artist. My dad is a factory worker and my mother is a housekeeper. No wonder I'm nervous."

Binky looked up at the navy and gold awning that covered the doorway to The Willows. There were shiny brass pots on either side of the imposing oak-and-glass doors. Binky tried to peek inside, but it was difficult to see through the heavily leaded beveled glass.

Binky gave a soft whimper, and Lexi looked at her in despair. "Binky, don't do this to yourself. These are just people. You're going for a simple job interview. You're not looking for them to adopt you!"

"Adopt me? They won't even hire me. They'll take one look at me and say, 'No way. Not for our precious child.' "

Binky had managed to convince herself that Mr.

and Mrs. Marlini, the owners of The Willows, were nearly perfect beings.

Lexi uttered a sound of disgust. "Binky, these people don't walk on water. Keep that in mind."

"No, I don't suppose they do, but they're certainly rich. You must admit that much. Look at this place!"

Binky finally managed to pull open the heavy door, and the girls moved into the dark, velvety foyer. It took a moment for their eyes to adjust to the dim light. If the outside had been imposing, the inside was even more so. Everything was done in rich burgundy velvet, dark oak and polished brass. The carpet on the floor was so plush that Lexi felt as though she were sinking into a foam cushion. The faint sounds of classical music drifted overhead. Even Lexi began to feel a sense of panic.

Suddenly, Harry Cramer appeared from behind a velvet drape. He almost stumbled in his surprise. "What are you girls doing here?"

"Binky's here for an interview," Lexi explained, "and she insisted that I come along—for moral support, I guess."

Harry grinned first at Binky and then at Lexi. "Yeah, I understand the feeling. This is a pretty awesome place the first time you see it. Let's go tell Mr. and Mrs. Marlini you're here."

Binky grabbed Harry's arm and hung on like a drowning victim. "No, no, not yet. Tell me what they're like. Tell me what I should say, Harry. Do I look all right? Have they had lots of applicants? Is there really any chance I can get this job?" Then she gave a small groan. "It's no use. I might as well just go home right now."

Harry laughed and patted Binky's small hand. "*Relax*, Binky. I haven't seen another applicant for this job. You'll be great."

He uncurled her fingers from the death grip they had on his arm and backed away. "You stay here. I'll go and get the Marlinis."

While he was gone, Binky paced back and forth and round and round, furiously spending her nervous energy. Meanwhile, Lexi searched for a place where she would be inconspicuous. She finally settled on a small bench just outside the coat room. In the dusky shadows of the restaurant, she would be practically invisible, yet close at hand for Binky—just in case.

"Miss McNaughton?" a woman's cultured voice said. "We're Mr. and Mrs. Marlini."

From Lexi's perch, she could see a handsome young couple not more than thirty-four or thirty-five years old approaching Binky. Mrs. Marlini had light blond hair, which flowed loosely around her shoulders, and her pale blue eyes had a dreamy expression. She was tall and slender and wore her clothes with the grace of a model.

Mr. Marlini was as dark and swarthy as his wife was fair. *He's quite handsome*, Lexi noted. His dark eyebrows met over the bridge of his nose, and he had a wise, but slightly artificial smile. His mannerisms were nervous, which made him look every bit as uncomfortable as Binky.

As he extended his hand toward Binky, Lexi noticed her friend take a small step backward before offering her own hand.

Maybe it's his eyebrows, Lexi thought to herself.

They did give him an angry look, even when he was smiling. But the couple was perfectly dressed and important looking.

Lexi saw Harry wink at Binky and then disappear behind a thick curtain. Now she was completely on her own.

"Tell me, Miss McNaughton," Mr. Marlini said as he looked Binky over from head to toe. "How old are you?"

"Uh, six—sixteen," Binky stammered, sounding much younger.

"And you feel that you're capable of watching a nine-year-old several evenings a week and on Saturdays?"

Binky nodded. "I've done lots of babysitting. I'm very used to children."

"And what kinds of things would you consider doing with our daughter the evenings while we're at work?"

Binky blinked and thought a moment before answering. "Well, I suppose we'd have to do homework first. If your daughter's nine, I'm sure she's starting to get a few assignments from her teachers. Maybe we could work together.

"Something I really liked doing when I was her age was working jigsaw puzzles. In fact, I have a collection of them. I have one-hundred piece puzzles, five-hundred piece, and even a five-thousand piece puzzle that I've been wanting to put together. Maybe your daughter would be interested in something like that. Or, we could read books or watch television.

"If she likes to do things in the kitchen, I make great fudge. I could teach her how and we could—"

"That all sounds very nice, Miss McNaughton. Tell me, what would you do if our daughter didn't express an interest in any of the things you've suggested?"

Binky looked taken aback. "Well, I suppose I would ask her what she'd like to do."

"Do you feel capable of disciplining a nine-year-old?"

Lexi frowned and shook her head as she listened. Surely a nine-year-old girl wouldn't need much discipline in a one-to-one setting! What kind of a child was this, anyway?

The question-and-answer session went on for several more minutes as Binky answered inquiries about her own background, her likes and dislikes, about her grades at school and even about her friends. Mr. Marlini did most of the questioning while his wife stood at his side, looking slightly bored.

Then abruptly, Mr. Marlini announced, "Well, I guess you'll do."

Binky blinked, slightly startled. "You mean I can have the job?"

"Of course. That's what I said."

Lexi, from her perch near the coat room, was equally surprised. Was that all there was to it? Didn't they want to check references or interview anyone else?

Before she had time to consider it further, a small girl came walking in from the back of the restaurant.

"Momma?" she said softly. "I was looking for you and—"

She stopped mid-sentence, suddenly shy when she saw a visitor.

The child was beautifully dressed in a coordinated outfit, making her look more like a little fashion plate than a child. Her hair was a rich dark blond that fell in soft curls below her shoulders, and her bangs were meticulously arranged and gelled into place. Her gray-green eyes looked serious and contemplative.

She was a very pretty child, Lexi noticed, but the expression on her face made her look wise beyond her years.

"Nicole?" Mrs. Marlini began, "I'd like you to meet Bonita McNaughton. Bonita will be your new babysitter. Bonita, this is Nicole."

Nicole studied Binky for a long moment. Hard as it was to imagine, the child actually looked afraid of Binky.

Binky stepped forward with her widest, most engaging smile. "Hello, Nicole. I'm glad to meet you. We're going to have a lot of fun together."

She was rewarded with a doubtful look. "Nicole, remember your manners," Mr. Marlini said abruptly.

From where she was sitting, Lexi saw the child glance at her father worriedly and then move closer to Binky.

"Nicole has difficulty in social situations," Mr. Marlini said with a hint of disgust in his voice. "Perhaps, Miss McNaughton, that is something you and the child will have to work on."

Binky nodded dutifully.

"Do you have any other questions, Miss McNaughton?"

"No, I don't think so. But you can call me Binky." Then she turned to Nicole. "I'd like it if you'd call me

Binky too. All my friends do."

Nicole nodded woodenly.

"I'm afraid you may have your hands full, Miss McNaughton," Mr. Marlini said. "Nicole is a very unresponsive child."

The distaste with which Mr. Marlini spoke of his daughter surprised everyone. Binky's cheeks flushed pink with embarrassment and Nicole blanched. Why, Lexi wondered to herself, would a father be so uncharitable about his own daughter in the presence of strangers?

Before she could consider it further, Mrs. Marlini, who had been quiet through most of the interview, stepped forward to say, "You can start on Saturday. Here's our home address. I've written it on the back of this business card. We'd like to be at the restaurant by ten, so if you can come about nine forty-five, that would be perfect."

"Nine forty-five?" Binky echoed. "Great."

If Binky had hoped to be rewarded with a smile from the child, she was disappointed. Nicole stared at her intently, her facial muscles tense and her eyes blank.

Abruptly, Mr. Marlini glanced at his watch. "If you'll excuse us, I believe we should get busy in the kitchen." He arched one of his close-set eyebrows, and his wife and Nicole turned and followed him mechanically toward the kitchen, leaving Binky standing in the foyer, looking forlorn and a little confused.

As soon as the family was out of sight, Harry appeared through the thick velvet curtains once again. "Well, that wasn't so bad, was it?"

"It was . . . weird," Binky finally managed. "Is

that how job interviews normally go?"

Harry chuckled. "No, but that's the way mine went. I think the Marlinis are different than most people."

Lexi joined them as they talked. "The man didn't seem very nice, somehow. That little girl certainly didn't look very happy."

Harry shook his head. "She never does. She's a really quiet child. When she's around the restaurant, she's always cowering in a corner. Of course, she gets into trouble if she does anything else."

Binky frowned. "I don't want her to be scared of me. If we're going to be together, I want us to have fun."

Lexi threw her arm around Binky's slender shoulders. "Then she's lucky she's getting you for a babysitter, Binky, because I know you'll make it fun for her. She'd be an even prettier little girl if she'd just smile."

Lexi stared at the door through which the Marlinis had vanished. "They're very strange people."

"They may be a little strange," Harry said softly, "but they're great cooks. I've been overhearing the customers the past few nights and it's been all praise. Sometimes, at the end of the evening, they allow the staff to take the leftovers." Harry licked his lips and rubbed his stomach. "Let me tell you, the food here is terrific!"

Somehow, the fact that Mr. and Mrs. Marlini were great cooks didn't soothe Lexi. She kept remembering Nicole's frightened gray-green eyes and the sharp tone with which her father had spoken to her.

Maybe she was being overly sensitive, Lexi reminded herself. Just because Lexi's own father never
raised his voice or spoke sharply didn't mean that
other fathers didn't or couldn't do that very thing.

Binky spoke up. "That little girl is too shy, that's
all I can say. I think my first job will be to work on
that." Binky's eyes twinkled. "Maybe I'll introduce
her to my brother Egg. It's hard to stay shy when
you meet Egg, don't you think? No one can feel insecure around a guy who looks like a stick figure and
eats rabbit food. Come on, let's get out of here."

As they walked down the street, Binky chattered
about all the ideas she had for bringing Nicole out
of her shell.

Mr. and Mrs. Marlini were very lucky, Lexi
thought to herself. Binky was going to be a great
babysitter.

Chapter Five

Lexi was eating lunch with Todd in the school cafeteria when Binky flung herself dramatically onto the bench beside them and announced, "You've *got* to help me!"

"Flunking math?" Todd asked mildly. "Or did you just get expelled?"

"Of course not!" Binky glared at him. "Lexi has to help me with my wardrobe."

"Oh. I knew it had to be something serious."

Ignoring Todd's sarcasm, Binky turned to Lexi. "Really, Lexi, I spent a half hour looking at my clothes this morning and I have nothing to wear to the circus!"

"But I thought Jennifer and I—"

"That was fine for the interview, but tonight at the circus I want to look really spectacular. Drop-dead gorgeous. You know!"

Lexi was prudent enough not to remind Binky that no matter what she did, her looks just didn't lend themselves to being "drop-dead gorgeous."

"Are you sure Harry is expecting a fashion model

tonight? Can't you just wear jeans and a sweatshirt? That's what I was planning to wear."

Binky looked pleadingly at Lexi. "It's my first real date! I want it to be special. Will you go shopping with me after school?"

"I thought you didn't have any money."

"I got a loan from Egg."

"What kind of interest rates is he asking?" Todd wondered.

"I do his share of the chores for a week."

Todd whistled through his teeth. "A loan shark too. Remind me never to borrow money from him."

"Dad said I didn't have to work at the veterinary clinic tonight," Lexi offered. "I suppose we could go to the mall right after school."

"And you could help me pick out something to wear!" Binky clapped her hands. "I'll see Jennifer next hour. I think I'll ask her if she wants to come along. I'll meet you at the south door right after the last class, okay?"

Lexi could hardly say no. Binky was moving forward with so much momentum that she wouldn't have paid any attention anyway. After she left, Todd put his hand over Lexi's. "Are you as excited as she is about going to the circus?"

She smiled into his eyes. "Of course. Can't you tell?"

He chuckled. "You hide it very well."

As Lexi stood up she turned to him with a teasing smile. "Who knows? I might just find something 'drop-dead gorgeous' to wear tonight."

———

Binky was dancing from one foot to the other when Lexi reached the south door of the school. Jennifer was already there, leaning casually against the wall, ignoring the spectacle Binky was making of herself.

"Ready?" Lexi asked.

"You're late, Lexi! I'll bet we'll miss the bus."

"There'll be another one."

"But we don't have much time. I need to do my hair when I get home."

"I'm glad she didn't get a date before this," Jennifer commented. "I couldn't have taken the pressure. Come on. I see the bus. We'll make it if we run."

———

The mall was unusually busy for a Friday afternoon. *Must have something to do with all the SALE signs in every store window*, Lexi decided.

"Where do we start? The Petite Shop? Junior Junction?"

"How about Junior Junction? That's where the Hi-Fives always go. Maybe they're having a good sale."

"Looks like the Hi-Fives have already been there," Jennifer pointed out. "Here comes Minda now."

Minda Hannaford was walking toward the threesome with an armload of packages. Tressa Williams and Mary Beth Adamson were only a few steps behind.

"So you're hitting the sales too," Minda said by way of greeting. "Sorry, there's nothing cute left. I think we bought it all."

"Oh, I think we'll manage to find something," Binky retorted cheerfully. "After all, I have Lexi helping me and she's great at putting clothes together."

"Since when did you care what you wore, Mc-Naughton? Have you been reading my fashion column, after all?"

Lexi stepped to Binky's side, forcing Minda to divide her attention between the two of them. "I think we'd better get going, Binky. After all, you need that new outfit for tonight. And you do want to have time to get ready for your date."

"You've got a date?" Minda's expression turned rabidly curious. "But who—"

"Well, we've got to go," Lexi said cheerfully as she and Jennifer steered Binky away from Minda's crowd. "Bye. Nice talking to you."

"A date! Dinky Binky McNaughton? Can you believe it? Who'd ask her out? Probably some nerd from the Science Club."

They had to walk several steps before Minda's curious jabbering could no longer be heard. As soon as they were out of earshot, Lexi and Jennifer broke into gales of laughter.

"Good for her! For once she got a real surprise!"

"The nerve of her! Why *shouldn't* Binky have a date?"

Suddenly Lexi noticed that Binky wasn't joining into their conversation. "Bink? Minda didn't get to you, did she?"

Binky turned to Lexi with an injured air. "Do you think she's right? Do you think that only nerds would want to ask me out?"

"Well, I think Harry Cramer is one of the *least* nerdy people I know. Besides, Minda had to say *something* mean. She can't stand it when a guy—any guy, even one she's not interested in—pays attention to a girl other than herself. You know Minda."

"Frankly," Jennifer added, "I think it's great that Minda found out you've got a date. She has this way of looking down at people that makes me sick."

Lexi gave Binky her most winning smile. "Besides, it's time that Minda realized that you're a very special person, Binky McNaughton!"

Binky's wavering smile grew stronger. "Hey, thanks, guys. I needed a pep talk."

"Anytime," Lexi assured her. "Now, I think we'd better go shopping."

As they turned into Junior Junction, Binky groaned. "Twenty percent off! I was hoping for at least thirty—or maybe even fifty! Egg didn't have all that much money to loan me!"

Lexi was already digging deep into the racks. Shortly she emerged with a pink and white jump suit. "How about this?"

Binky barely glanced at it. "Too expensive. I can tell."

"No, it's not. It's been marked down four times. I'll bet it's because it's such a small size. Try it on. It would be perfect with that pair of hot pink sandals you have."

"You think so?" Binky said hesitantly.

Lexi thrust the outfit into her hands. "Absolutely."

"Whew! That was fast!" Jennifer observed as they emerged from the Junior Junction. "You found exactly the right outfit in less than twenty minutes!"

"Thanks to Lexi." Binky clutched the large white bag. "I love it too."

Lexi glanced at her watch. "Well, you've still got time and money to spend. What next?"

"How about a new hairdo?" Jennifer suggested. "Something really special."

"Oh, I don't think so."

"We can loan you some money until your first paycheck," Jennifer offered. "You really do need a new look to go with that jump suit."

"But . . ."

"I think Jennifer's right," Lexi added. "My mom goes to a little shop somewhere in this mall that she says is great. I'm going there next time I need a cut. Want to see if they have any walk-in openings?"

"Maybe if I put my hair up like Jennifer fixed it the other day . . ."

"This is your big moment, Bink. A first date. How often does that happen?"

"Well . . ."

By the time they'd walked the length of the mall, Lexi and Jennifer had convinced Binky that a new look was exactly what she needed. Before she could change her mind, she was sitting in the hairdresser's chair staring nervously into the mirror.

"We'll wait out front, Binky," Jennifer said.

Binky nodded mutely, not quite sure of this new turn of events but unwilling to back out now.

In the waiting room, which smelled of fruit-scented shampoo, Lexi and Jennifer sat down to wait.

Jennifer was quiet for a long time before speaking. "I hope Binky likes her new job."

Lexi glanced up from the magazine she was reading. "Why shouldn't she?"

"I don't know exactly. My parents ate at The Willows last week."

"Didn't they like it?"

"Yeah. They said the food was wonderful."

"So? What's the problem?"

"They were with friends who knew the people who run the restaurant."

"The Marlinis?"

"Yeah. They were neighbors for a while before the Marlinis moved." Jennifer was thoughtful, as if she were choosing her words very carefully. "My parents' friends said that Mr. Marlini had a very bad temper."

Lexi remembered Mr. Marlini's intense look and impatient questions. "Do you think he might lose his temper with Binky?"

"I don't know. My parents were talking about this, and I listened because I knew Harry Cramer was working for them, that's all."

"Well, I don't think you should mention this to Binky," Lexi advised, "at least not until she's had a chance to form her own opinions about Mr. and Mrs. Marlini."

"You're probably right. I don't want her to be nervous about her job now." Finally Jennifer grinned. "Otherwise, she'll have you and me over there holding her hand while she works!"

They were laughing at the idea when Binky emerged from the back of the salon.

"Bink? Is that you?"

Binky grinned and touched the tips of her attractively styled hair with her fingers. "Do you like it?"

Her reddish brown hair hung down her back in a graceful french braid, her bangs falling into a mass of soft curls. The hairdo was everything it should be. It made Binky look taller, prettier, even older.

"It's perfect!"

"Do you really think so?"

"Definitely! Harry is going to love it!"

Binky glanced anxiously at her watch. "Harry! That reminds me! Lexi, we're supposed to get ready for the circus!"

When Lexi arrived home, her little brother Ben was helping her father in the front yard. Dr. Leighton was trimming hedges and Ben was dutifully stuffing the trimmed branches into a big garbage bag. Ben had also managed to spread leaves all over the yard.

"I'm helping, Lexi!" he announced proudly. "See?"

"You're doing great, Ben. Looks good." Lexi ruffled his silky brown hair.

Ben returned her smile with a wide one of his own and his brown almond-shaped eyes danced. Ben's sunny disposition always cheered Lexi.

As she watched Ben and her father clear up the last of the twigs, Lexi felt a rush of gratitude. "Thanks, God," she murmured. "Thanks for all my family."

She really was blessed, Lexi knew. She had no money worries like Binky because she worked for her father in the clinic, feeding animals and answering the phone. She had parents who were able to support her and a little brother who, though he could irritate her with his teasing, didn't eat tofu burgers and lift weights.

Lexi hummed as she got ready for the evening. After all the fuss over Binky's wardrobe, she decided to wear a pair of simple white slacks and a bright blue top. No use competing with Binky tonight. She deserved her special moment.

She'd just finished supper when Lexi heard Todd's car pull up to the curb. He was halfway up the steps when she reached the door. Todd looked wonderful, as usual. His dark blond hair was still damp from the shower and Lexi could see the little tracks where he'd run his hands through it. Harry waited in the car.

"Ready?"

"I am. I hope Binky is!"

"I got the impression she was nervous about to-night."

"You have that right," Lexi smiled, "but wait until you see her!"

"She looks good?"

"Very good!"

Chapter Six

As they neared the McNaughton house, they could see Egg jogging down the street. He was wearing running shorts, knee-hi socks and tennis shoes. He had ear plugs in his ears and a small portable radio hooked to his belt. His face was flushed to a bright red and the rest of his body was splotched with pink. The sweat was running down his forehead and into his eyes. Every few seconds he lifted his hand to flick the moisture away. His arms and legs were still dreadfully thin and gangly.

He reminded Lexi of the cardboard jointed skeleton that her mother always dragged out the week before Halloween. "Mr. Bones," Ben always called it. Well, today, as he loped down the sidewalk, Egg looked very much like Mr. Bones himself.

"I see Egg's jogging," Harry smiled.

"Among other things. He's also lifting weights. Egg's trying to bulk up."

Harry chuckled. "Well, he could use a little bulking, I suppose, but Egg's just not a muscular body type. I don't think he'll ever be satisfied if he gets it in his head that he's going to be Mr. America. He's got runners' muscles, not weight lifters' muscles."

The two boys launched into a long conversation about weight training. Suddenly, Lexi was very eager to have Binky join her in the car to help her steer the conversation in some other direction.

As Harry started up the walk, Binky came out of the house, and Lexi strained to catch Harry's expression. She was pleased to see that he thought Binky looked absolutely terrific.

As they headed for the Convention Center, Harry struggled for the right words. "I never thought, Binky. I mean I never expected . . ." Then he blurted, "You look wonderful. Do you know that?"

Binky, who had been covertly studying her reflection in the car window, smiled. "Lexi and Jennifer thought I needed a new look."

Harry nodded emphatically, "Well, I liked your old look, but this one is pretty spectacular."

Todd and Lexi grinned at each other. It was apparent that Harry and Binky were fast becoming a mutual admiration society.

The Cedar River Convention Center was a massive concrete building near the center of town. Its distinctive shape and meticulously kept landscaping saved it from being a cement eyesore. Instead, the Convention Center grounds had become a favorite spot of Cedar River residents, who often came to picnic in the surrounding parks. Tonight, there were dozens of families doing just that while they waited for the circus to begin.

"The doors are open," Harry announced to no one in particular. "We might as well go in and get situated."

The closer they walked to the Convention Center doors, the more they could hear the sounds of the circus inside. There were elephants trumpeting loudly within the building, and Lexi could hear the muffled roar of a tiger. There were horses and llamas and one small billy goat grazing outside the center as they walked by. A clown in a baggy red-and-white suit with an orange nose and green hair waddled by and tipped his imaginary hat as they entered the building. Inside, the foursome was assaulted with the sounds and the smells of the circus.

"Oooh." Binky gave a little gasp. "Fresh roasted peanuts. Can you smell them?"

"And cotton candy," Todd added. "It's just not a circus without getting some of that stuck all over your clothes and face." Then he glanced at the long line forming behind the ticket counter. "Maybe I'd better go and stand in line for the tickets while you guys look around."

Harry and Binky nodded enthusiastically and headed toward a vender selling helium-inflated balloons the shape of alligators and submarines. Lexi, meanwhile, followed Todd through the line.

"Something tells me they'd like to be alone," she said with a smile.

Todd chuckled. "It's a good thing we're along to chaperon," he commented, only half in jest.

By the time Todd and Lexi's line had reached the ticket office and they had purchased the tickets, Harry and Binky returned. Binky was carrying a pink-and-gray balloon—an elephant dressed in a little net tutu. She was wearing a clown hat with a purple pom-pom, and in her other hand she had cotton candy.

There was no point in asking if she was having fun, Lexi thought to herself. That was written all over Binky's face.

"Do you want anything?" Todd wondered and looked at Lexi. "It looks like Binky's all set for the circus already."

"Some popcorn would be fine," Lexi said. "I don't think I want an elephant in a pink tutu, yet."

"Okay, suit yourself. Why don't we find our seats and then I'll come back for the popcorn."

Todd returned just as the ringmaster came into the illuminated middle ring, cracking his whip and announcing loudly, "Ladies and Gentlemen of Cedar River. Welcome to. . . ."

As he gave the full greeting, a dog act appeared in the ring at the far side of the arena. Twirling lights settled high above the ground on a tight-rope walker in the center ring. Lexi heard Binky give a little gasp.

"It's her!" she murmured.

"Do you know her?" Lexi asked, astounded, wondering where Binky could have met her.

"No. We saw her out in the hall, didn't we, Harry? She looks so different up there."

"Different? How?"

Binky shrugged her shoulders, her eyes glued on the woman cavorting on the middle of the tight-rope wire. "Out in the hallway, she was talking to some kids and she looked so old. Her face was all lined and her makeup was too heavy. She looked more like a raccoon than a human being. She had a lot of gray in her hair and those mesh tights she's wearing? Well, there was a big hole and a run in one of them all the way down the side of her leg. Still," and Binky stared even harder at the woman tripping lightly along the wire, "up there, she looks perfectly wonderful. You can't see any of the wrinkles or the gray hair or the runs or anything. From a distance, and with all those lights on that beautiful sparkling costume, she looks just perfect."

Harry nodded. "I guess that just proves things aren't always as they seem. She looked shabby close up, but," and he shrugged his shoulders, "she looks great up there."

Things aren't always as they seem.

Lexi had learned that at a very young age. Ben had been a beautiful, lovable baby and it had been hard to imagine then that he would never grow up to be normal. Now, people who didn't know him saw only the fact that he was retarded, not that he was a loving, affectionate, charming human being. Lexi's parents often pointed out that things *aren't* always what they seem.

There was only one steady and true constant life Lexi knew. That was Jesus Christ. He was always what He promised to be.

Lexi smiled to herself. It was an odd thought to be having at the circus, she supposed: But, her parents encouraged her to allow Jesus to be part of every portion of her life, the fun times as well as the sad times. So probably it wasn't so odd, after all, to be thinking about Him here in the middle of the bright lights, flashing colors and excitement.

Six elephants came loping into the arena and entered the far ring. The lead elephant was lifting his trunk and bellowing like a mighty trumpet. Following him and clinging to his tail was a slightly smaller elephant. And so it went, down to the last elephant— a baby, clutching the tail of the elephant in front of him. And behind the baby there was a clown with green hair, lunging clumsily for the baby elephant's tail, falling flat on his face, then scrambling to his feet and lunging again.

From that moment on, Lexi and her friends were caught up in the activity of the circus.

After the show, as they made their way toward the outside doors, Binky tugged on Harry's sleeve. "Hang on a minute. I want to stop at one of these stands and buy something."

"You can't want more cotton candy," Harry teased. "And you've already got a balloon, a hat, two flags and a T-shirt!"

Binky shook her head. "Not for me, silly. It's for Nicole."

"Who's Nicole?" Todd wondered.

"She's the little girl I'm going to be babysitting," Binky explained. "I saw a coloring book here. It might be a bit childish for her, but it has some good pictures of the high-wire artist and the clown. Don't you think it might be a nice gesture if I brought her something on my first day with her?"

"I think that sounds like a great idea," Lexi enthused. "But why not give her something you already have? Like that elephant in the tutu?"

"No way." Binky secured the elephant balloon protectively. "These are my souvenirs. I'm going to get Nicole something of her own."

It was no wonder Binky was always broke, Lexi thought to herself. She was usually very lavish with whatever money she had. Perhaps this job would give her a chance to manage her money more responsibly.

As they walked toward the car, Binky handed her souvenir treasures to Harry and gripped her stomach. "Ooooh," she moaned weakly.

"Something wrong?"

"It must be all the cotton candy," she murmured, looking suddenly pale. "I haven't eaten much else today, and all that sugar on an empty stomach is making me feel sick."

"How about a burger at the Hamburger Shack?" Todd asked. "Do you think that would help settle things down?"

Binky nodded. Her face was turning paler by the minute, and Lexi could see her lips tensing up. Fortunately, even with the heavy traffic, Todd was able to maneuver his '49 Ford out of the parking lot and onto the highway with little difficulty. They were at the Hamburger Shack in less than five minutes.

Jerry Randle was working behind the counter, making malts and spooning nuts onto banana splits. Several girls from the Hi-Fives were in their customary booth at the back, and there was the usual pack of boys vying for their attention.

Minda Hannaford sat in the center of the group, looking coy and very self-satisfied.

"Minda's holding court again, I see," Todd whispered into Lexi's ear as he nodded toward the back of the restaurant. Todd understood Minda as well as anyone. He had even dated her for a short time.

Minda was a very troubled and troubling girl. It was difficult to maintain any sort of meaningful relationship with her. Lexi had found that out the hard way when she first moved to Cedar River.

Minda's attention turned to the four who had just entered the restaurant. Her blue eyes widened and her normally pouty lips fell open in surprise. Lexi felt a nudge of satisfaction as Minda stared openly at Binky and Harry Cramer. Harry, in the eyes of the Hi-Fives, was considered a good catch. Lexi knew through the school grapevine that the Hi-Five girls had a rating system for boys in the school; and on their scale of one to five, Harry was definitely a four or above.

Lexi glanced through lowered lashes at her friend Binky, who was in animated conversation with Harry about the remote probability of getting fifteen large clowns in a Volkswagen. She hadn't even noticed Minda and her crowd. Binky's eyes were dancing, and her new hairdo and outfit made her appear so much more stylish and mature than before. For once, instead of looking three years younger than she actually was, Binky looked her age—a very pretty sixteen.

Todd nudged Lexi. "Look at Minda," he whispered. There was a chuckle in his voice. Minda was still staring at them. Then she turned to Tressa Williams who was seated at her right. Lexi could read her lips, "Is that *Binky*?" Tressa nodded in amazement.

"So Minda *can* be taken down a peg or two," Todd said. "I think she's really impressed with the new Binky."

"Minda's been cruel to Binky so many times, I've lost count," Lexi retorted softly. "I'm glad for once she's seeing Binky as she really can be—attractive and popular."

Todd shrugged. "I suppose. Still, it's Minda who has the problem. She hasn't learned that what people are on the inside is what counts. The outward appearance isn't worth much if the inside—what one feels and thinks—isn't what it should be."

Lexi looked at Todd with renewed affection and admiration. Todd was absolutely right. That's why she valued his friendship so much, because he could always put things into proper perspective. He knew what was important. He knew that the most beautiful face in the world could hide the ugliest disposition—but not for very long.

In fact, his idea was the same one expressed in the Bible passage Lexi had been reading only yesterday. She'd found it in Matthew 23:

> Woe to you, scribes and Pharisees, hypocrites! for you cleanse the outside of the cup and of the plate, but inside they are full of extortion and rapacity.
>
> You blind Pharisee! first cleanse the inside of the cup and of the plate, that the outside also may be clean.
>
> Woe to you, scribes and Pharisees, hypocrites! for you are like whitewashed tombs, which outwardly appear beautiful, but within they are full of dead men's bones and all uncleanness. So you also outwardly appear righteous to men, but within you are full of hypocrisy and iniquity.

Lexi remembered the verses because she'd had to look in the dictionary for the word *rapacity*. She learned it meant greediness. But, more than that, it was God's condemnation of men who pretended to be clean and perfect on the outside but were really full of greed and sin.

"Let's take the table over by the window," Harry suggested. "We'd better sit down before everyone who was at the circus decides it's time for something more to eat."

Lexi was glad that Harry and Binky sat with their backs toward Minda and her gang. That way they couldn't see the staring glances that were coming their way.

After they had ordered, Todd leaned back in the booth, crossing his arms on his chest. "So, Harry, how's the new job going?"

"Oh, it's all right, I guess," Harry said quietly.

"You don't sound very enthusiastic," Todd pointed out.

"Don't I? I don't mean to sound unappreciative or anything. It's a good job. They pay well and I was lucky to get it."

"But, how do you like it?"

"The people in the back are pretty nice," Harry said. "I've met a couple of guys who are working there while going to college that are really great. We've talked about going golfing sometime."

"Seems to me you're evading my question."

Harry grinned sheepishly. "I guess I am. I just don't want to scare Binky before she starts working for the Marlinis."

"Scare me?" Binky said. "What's that supposed to mean?"

"The Marlinis are perfectionists, that's all," Harry said by way of an explanation. "They're very fussy. And they're very, very strict. They set up rules and they expect everyone to obey them to the letter or else."

"Or else what?" Binky wondered.

Harry shrugged. "I guess I really don't know. No one ever dares to cross Mr. Marlini to find out."

"It's the eyebrows," Binky said abruptly. "There's no break in them over the bridge of his nose. They look like one big slash. They make him look mean, don't they?"

Harry laughed out loud. "Maybe you're right, Binky. Maybe it *is* the eyebrows. Anyway, Mr. Marlini has everyone scared into obeying his rules, that's all I can say." He paused thoughtfully for a moment before adding, "They're pretty impatient, too. Both of them. Although I think Mr. Marlini is worse. When they say they want something done, they want it done immediately, not two seconds from now."

Binky whistled through her teeth. "I'm glad you're telling me this. It's probably good that I know. That way, I won't get into any trouble with Nicole."

"Poor kid," Todd said. "It must be tough to live with parents who are like that all the time."

Harry nodded. "Yeah, they want everything done just right. No room for error. I've seen them discipline an employee because the silverware wasn't aligned perfectly on the table." He glanced at Binky warily as if he were considering his next words. Finally, he said, "I've even seen Mr. Marlini punish Nicole because she was told to pick up her toys and she overlooked a book that had gotten caught in the chair cushion."

"But that could happen to anyone," Binky protested.

Harry nodded. "My point exactly. I really don't understand. It's kinda weird, because Mr. and Mrs.

Marlini are wonderful chefs. I mean, the customers absolutely rave about the food. Still, they act insecure about other things. Do you understand what I'm saying?"

"Not exactly," Binky said, her brow furrowed in puzzlement.

"Well, they get everybody to do everything perfectly, the restaurant's immaculate, the food is super and all the customers think they're great, yet, it's still not good enough. Hey, they're working with imperfect human beings, after all."

"Maybe they're just nervous because they're starting a new business," Todd suggested. "According to my mom and dad, that's a pretty tough thing to do in this day and age."

"I suppose that could be it," Harry said.

They ate in silence for a few minutes, and then suddenly Harry spoke again. "You know, when I think about it, I don't think the Marlinis trust anyone."

Lexi, Todd and Binky all stared at him. "Huh?"

"They don't trust anyone. They don't trust us to do our work the way we should. They don't trust us enough to talk to any of us about the business. They don't seem to have any real friends they can count on either."

"Who'd want to be their friends if they're so fussy?" Binky wondered.

Harry nodded. "Yeah. I certainly wouldn't want to be their child either."

"What do you mean by that?" Lexi mused.

"Oh, it's just that they demand letter-perfect behavior from their daughter, just like everyone else. She's only a kid."

"Does she have any grandparents she could talk to?" Lexi wondered. Lexi's own grandparents were wonderful sounding boards when she was a child.

"Not that I know of. They're really loners. They don't seem to have much to do with their neighbors, and I've never heard them mention family."

"Poor kid," Todd said. "Sounds like a rotten way to grow up. No grandparents or friends. Just hanging around the restaurant with adults, getting into trouble for every little thing. Doesn't sound like much of a life to me."

Then Harry shrugged. "I don't know; maybe it's all right. Nicole probably doesn't know any differently. Anyway, I can't imagine her ever doing anything wrong. Sometimes she's so quiet we forget she's there. I've seen her fall asleep under a chair in the kitchen and spend the whole evening there."

"Well, then they really do need me," Binky announced. "I'll certainly be better for her than hanging around the restaurant, not having any fun at all."

Lexi recognized the determined thrust of Binky's chin. Now, not only did she have a job, she had a cause. Nicole Marlini was going to get the very best of Binky's attention. That thought was oddly comforting to Lexi. She felt sorry for this little girl she didn't even know.

With a gasp, Binky stared at her watch. "Do you realize what time it is?" she said to no one in particular. "My job starts tomorrow! I've got to get home!"

"Well, Binky," Todd said with a smile, "I think you'll be a great employee with your attitude!"

Binky grinned. "Well, maybe you and Harry can

put in a good word about me to Mr. Marlini—about my dedication and loyalty, my beauty, my intelligence and grace—"

"And your modesty?" Todd finished for her.

All four of them were laughing as they left the Hamburger Shack.

Chapter Seven

It was after ten A.M. by the time Lexi opened one drowsy eyelid and peered at the clock on her bedside stand. She yawned, stretched mightily and curled back into a ball under her covers for a moment before resigning herself to the fact that it really was time to get up. After tugging on her robe and sliding her slippers out from beneath her bed, she made her way down the stairs to the kitchen.

Ben was seated at the kitchen counter intently watching a cartoon—one that Lexi remembered as a favorite of hers when she was his age. He was also stuffing powdered sugar donuts into his mouth, one after the other.

Mrs. Leighton was busy on the other side of the kitchen. Lexi peered into the pot of Italian sauce bubbling on the stove.

"Mmmmm, lasagna?" she said.

"For dinner tonight. How does that sound?"

"Not so good right now, but it'll be great later. Is Ben eating the last of the donuts?"

"It appears that way," Mrs. Leighton said, looking amused. "It's a good thing I don't have them around very often, the way he inhales them."

Lexi yawned and shuffled to the refrigerator. She took out the orange juice and poured a large glass for herself. Then, rummaging a little deeper, she found a package of bagels. Methodically, she split one and popped it into the toaster. When it was warm, she spread it with a light coating of cream cheese and sat down on one of the stools near Ben.

"Well," she wondered aloud, "I wonder how Binky's doing?"

Her mother looked at her expectantly. "Doing about what?"

"Today's the first day of her new job babysitting for Nicole Marlini."

"That's right. You did mention that Binky had found a nanny position."

"She's nervous, too," Lexi confided. "From what we've gathered, the Marlinis are very particular and very strict."

"How many children do they have?"

"Just one. She's nine."

"Well, that shouldn't be too hard," Mrs. Leighton commented. "Binky's accustomed to lots of children."

"I know. In fact, she's probably more used to a whole bunch of noisy, rowdy ones than one quiet little girl like Nicole. Harry says the girl's mom and dad expect perfection from her, too."

"Who's Harry and how would he know what they expect?" her mother wondered.

"Oh, Harry's the boy that Binky went to the circus with last night. He works for the Marlinis too.

He seems to know more about them than anyone else."

"All this talk about restaurants makes me think it's time your father took me out for dinner again. What do you think about that, Lexi?"

Ben, from his position in front of the television set, said, "Out for dinner. Let's go."

"Aren't you full of donuts?" Lexi smiled as she pointed to a little heap of powdered sugar right in front of Ben at the counter.

"Full," Ben said regretfully. Then he clambered off his stool. "Ben will work it off," he announced and bolted for the back door.

"Where did he get that?" Mrs. Leighton remarked.

Lexi laughed. "I think he overheard Todd and Egg talking about it one night. One of them had one too many milk shakes and said he would have to work it off."

Just as her mother was about to respond, the doorbell rang and Jennifer Golden peeked her head in the door. "Hello. Anybody home?" She sauntered in without waiting for an invitation and gave Lexi an up-and-down stare. "You just get out of bed?" she quipped. "I've been up for hours." Then she reached for a glass, poured her own orange juice and helped herself to the other half of Lexi's bagel.

"Make yourself at home," Lexi chuckled.

"Thanks, I think I will. So, how was the circus?"

Lexi grinned broadly. "Great. Binky and Harry had a wonderful time. Afterward we went to the Hamburger Shack, and Minda Hannaford got to see who Binky was out with."

Jennifer's face lit up. "I bet she almost croaked!"

"You girls certainly aren't being very charitable to Minda," Mrs. Leighton reminded them. "I do understand how Minda can be, but unkindness toward her won't help."

"We're not being unkind, Mom, we're just glad that for once Minda didn't have an excuse to laugh at Binky."

"So, what are your plans for today?" Jennifer asked, changing the subject.

Lexi looked at the clock. "I have chores I promised to do at my dad's clinic. I need to wash out all the cages that aren't occupied. There's also a delivery that needs to be checked off."

"I could come along and help you," Jennifer offered. "You'd get done in half the time."

"Are you sure you want to spend your Saturday doing that?" Lexi wondered.

Jennifer shrugged, "Why not? I really haven't anything better to do."

"Well, if you say so. I could use the help." Lexi pushed herself away from the counter. "Just wait until I pull on some jeans and a T-shirt and we'll be on our way."

Though Dr. Leighton did keep Saturday morning office hours, the clinic was quiet. There was only one lady in the waiting room with a small blue parakeet in a big silver cage.

Lexi could hear her father talking softly in one of the examining rooms and an occasional woof reverberated down the hall.

"My father should be with you in just a moment,"

Lexi told the women clutching her cage. "It sounds as if there's only one patient ahead of you."

The woman nodded nervously. "I found him lying on the bottom of his cage this morning." She looked anxiously at the budgie. "What do you think it could be?"

Lexi smiled. "I don't know, but I'm sure my dad will. He's a great vet."

The woman nodded. "Yes, I've heard that. My neighbor has a pair of Pekingese who have been here several times."

"Oh, do you mean Pip and Squeak?" Lexi said with a smile. "I know them."

The older woman's face relaxed. "My, you do give personalized service here, don't you?"

Lexi chuckled. "I'm Dr. Leighton's daughter. I've just come in to do some chores. If there's anything I can get for you, just let me know."

After checking off the delivery, it took only fifteen minutes for Jennifer and Lexi to scrub out the empty cages. In another ten, they were finished feeding the animals. When Lexi and Jennifer went back to the front desk, the lady and her parakeet were gone.

Deftly, Lexi opened the mail and arranged it in piles for her father—reading literature in one pile; bills in another; personal mail in a third.

Jennifer hoisted herself to the top of the desk and sat there watching Lexi. She swung one leg back and forth, and chewed thoughtfully on a wad of gum. "I wonder how Binky's doing this morning," Jennifer said finally.

Lexi looked up at her friend. "I've been thinking the same thing. You know how Binky is. Sometimes she tries so hard to do everything perfectly that she ends up botching it all."

"How bad can it be?" Jennifer wondered. "One little girl just can't be that much trouble." She glanced at her watch. "Oh-oh. I promised my mom I'd be home by now. I'd better be going."

"Thanks for your help," Lexi called as Jennifer disappeared through the office door. "Talk to you later."

Jennifer waved back over her head without turning around.

It took Lexi only a few moments more to finish up the jobs she'd started. She returned home on her bike to find Ben on the front porch sitting in the swing, chanting to himself: "Phone's for Lexi. Phone's for Lexi."

"Hi, Ben. What are you doing?"

"Phone's for you, Lexi," Ben announced.

"Right now? There's someone on the phone for me?"

"All morning," Ben said with great emphasis.

Mrs. Leighton walked out onto the porch. "There you are. Binky's called several times. I was hoping you'd get home soon. She seems more and more distraught each time she calls."

"Oh?" Lexi frowned. This didn't sound good. From the interior of the house, Lexi heard the phone ring again.

It was Binky, her voice tinny and far away.

"Lexi? Where have you been?"

"I've been working at my dad's clinic," Lexi explained. "Mom said you've been calling."

"You've got to help me, Lexi. I don't know what

to do. Nicole is so shy that she'll hardly talk to me. I'm having a terrible time finding ways to entertain her. All she does is sit in the corner of the couch and stare at me with those big gray-green eyes."

"She needs a little time, that's all," Lexi began.

"Time? She's had all morning. The only words I've heard her say are 'No, thank-you.' She doesn't want to eat. She doesn't want to play. She just wants to sit on the corner of the couch and stare at me with those big sad eyes. You've got to come over, Lexi. Help me out. This is going to be the first and last day of my job if I can't do any better than this."

Lexi chewed thoughtfully on her upper lip. *Poor Binky. Could I really be of any help?*

"Lexi? Are you coming?" Binky pleaded.

With a sigh, Lexi asked for the address.

She swung onto her bike and rode quickly to the address Binky had given her. The Marlini house was really lovely, Lexi observed. It was situated on a quiet, winding street. The house was nestled in a small grove of trees, isolated from its neighbors by a huge expanse of grass and shrubbery.

"Impressive," Lexi murmured. The house was as every bit as imposing as The Willows restaurant. She kicked out the bike stand and parked her bike at the foot of the stairs that led to the front door. She rang the doorbell once and was about to ring it again when the small girl with soft dark blond curls came to the door. The child's expression was serious, her grey-green eyes almost accusing.

"Hi, Nicole," Lexi began.

The child's steady gaze startled her. It was as though adult eyes were staring at her from a child's body. The little girl opened the door widely and indicated that Lexi should come in.

Nicole was perfectly groomed, as neat as the inside of the house. Lexi wanted to look around and take in this amazingly beautiful home, but the most important task seemed to be attention to this small, intense child before her.

"I hear you and Binky have been getting to know each other this morning," Lexi said cheerfully. "I'm Lexi Leighton, Binky's friend." She held out her hand. The child took it and shook it somberly, but did not smile.

Just then, Binky came fluttering into the room. "Hi, Lexi. I'm so glad you could come. I've told Nicole all about you and I know she wanted to meet you." Binky's voice was bright, brittle and artificial. Her smile was forced. Lexi could read the panic in Binky's eyes. Things were not going well at all.

"You live in a very lovely home, Nicole," Lexi said to the girl.

"Why don't we all go into the other room," Binky suggested. "We could visit and get to know each other better."

The threesome entered the cavernous living room. The ceilings were vaulted, reaching to a height of twelve feet. The fireplace that graced one entire wall was made of dark field stone and grouted with black mortar. It was a forbidding looking room, Lexi thought to herself, dark and serious, much like the child's personality.

Along one wall was an entertainment center with a big-screen TV and a dozen electronic gadgets that looked highly impressive and complicated.

Lexi turned to Nicole. "Shall we listen to some music? What a great stereo system you have."

Nicole looked frightened. "I can't."

"You can't listen to music?" Lexi echoed. "Really?"

"I can't touch the stereo," Nicole said.

Lexi glanced at the complex equipment. "I guess I can understand that. Do you have a little record player in your room? That would be fine. Or a tape player?"

Nicole shook her head somberly. "Just this. But you can't touch it."

It was a settled issue with the child that she couldn't listen to music because she couldn't touch the equipment.

So Binky tried another tactic. "How about puzzles? Sometimes when Lexi and I are bored, we do a puzzle. That's a lot of fun."

"I can't," she answered sadly. It seemed these words were quite common in Nicole's vocabulary.

"Why not?" Binky said impatiently. Lexi could tell that she was just about at the end of her rope.

"My dad says I'm too old for puzzles."

"For baby puzzles, maybe," Binky said with exasperation, "but not for big puzzles. Why, we could get a thousand-piece one that Lexi and I have worked."

"My dad says I'm too old for puzzles" was the plaintive reply.

There was no point in pursuing the issue. The child was not allowed to listen to music or to do a simple puzzle. She looked at Binky impatiently as if to say, "Don't you understand the rules here?"

Now Lexi understood Binky's problem. Nicole was fearful of doing anything that might displease her strict father.

"How about a walk?" Lexi blurted, at a loss to suggest anything else. Nicole looked at her steadily for a moment. Finally she said, "My dad didn't say anything about walks."

"Well, that must mean he won't mind if you take one," Binky concluded. "Get a sweater and we'll go outside. You've got such a beautiful yard. Maybe you can show us what's out there."

Dutifully, Nicole hurried away to get her sweater. When they were alone, Binky and Lexi stared at each other. Binky grabbed Lexi's hand and said, "I'm so glad you're here. You see my problem, don't you?"

"I certainly do. What an odd child." Lexi shook her head in amazement. "I'm not advocating diso-bedience to parents, but don't her father's demands seem a bit out of line?"

"They sure do. After I called you, she and I started to talk a little bit and she said some very unusual things."

"Oh? What sort of unusual things?"

Binky gave Lexi a bewildered look. "After I called you and had hung up the phone, Nicole rearranged it on the phone stand. She said her father didn't like anything out of place. Then she tripped on the cord and the phone fell and landed on her foot."

"Ouch," Lexi said. "That must have hurt."

"But you should have heard what she said!" She repeated the words the child had spoken.

Lexi's eyes widened. "Where did a nine-year-old pick up that kind of language?"

Binky shrugged. "I don't know, but at my house, we'd get our mouths washed out with soap if we said anything like that."

Lexi nodded. Surely Nicole hadn't heard her father say such words! Or had she?

Nicole returned then, preventing Lexi and Binky from continuing their conversation.

She led the way into the park-like backyard, and the three girls walked among the flowers. An occasional squirrel skittering through the tree branches seemed to enchant Nicole. For the first time, Lexi saw her smile.

What was wrong with this child, anyway? Lexi wondered. She'd never seen anyone quite so shy. Nicole was as nervous and timid as the little red squirrel playing on the branch overhead. It was okay to watch him, but the little creature would never allow anyone to touch him. How very much like the animal was this young frightened girl!

"Let's go for a walk to the end of the block and back," Binky suggested. Then she patted her pocket. "I even have some change with me. Maybe we could stop somewhere for an ice cream cone."

For once, Nicole didn't say "I can't." Instead, she walked solemnly between Binky and Lexi as the older girls led the way.

"Oooh, we aren't very far from the library, Nicole," Binky pointed out. "I like books, don't you?"

Nicole gave her a blank, uncomprehending stare.

"Would you like to go there someday? Maybe we could check out some books."

Nicole's expression brightened. "Really? I love books."

Binky gave Lexi a triumphant look over the top of Nicole's head as if to say, "Finally, something we have in common."

"What kind of books do you like, Nicole?" Binky asked.

"I like horse stories a lot," she said. "*Black Beauty* is my favorite—and mysteries. I like them too. But, I don't like scary books. I can't sleep when I read scary books." Nicole was off and running, telling about the characters in this book and that and listing one by one her all-time favorite stories.

Binky and Lexi were both smiling along with Nicole when they returned to the Marlini house with their ice cream.

Lexi glanced at her watch. "I think I'd better be going now."

Binky nodded. "Thanks for coming, Lexi. Nicole and I will be just fine now. Since we both like to read, I think we've found something to talk about."

Lexi let herself quietly out the front door. She could hear Nicole and Binky enthusiastically discussing the merits of choose-your-own-ending-adventure books. Lexi smiled as she swung onto her bike and started for home.

Nicole was definitely an odd child, but she was sweet too. Lexi liked the way her eyes lit up with excitement when she started talking about her books. It was too bad so few things seem to spark her energy that way. Still, now that she and Binky had a common ground to start from, Lexi had no doubt that Binky would be able to draw Nicole out of her shell.

As Lexi entered her own house, she heard loud

roaring sounds coming from the living room where Ben had set up an entire race track. He was making all the roaring and crashing sounds that accompany any exciting race.

Mrs. Leighton put her hands over her ears and shook her head, "Your brother seems to have only one volume today, and that's loud! I've been hearing the Indy 500 coming out of the living room for almost two hours. I don't mind the roaring of the motors; but when they crash, Ben makes almost more noise than I can tolerate."

Just then Lexi heard Ben screech and pile two cars into each other with an accompanied "Boom! Crash! Bang!"

"I see what you mean," Lexi said with a smile. "But actually, I kind of enjoy it." Her mother stared at her in amazement.

So what if Ben is loud and noisy? Lexi thought as she left the room. She definitely preferred his noise to Nicole Marlini's grim silence.

Chapter Eight

"Nicole and I are going shopping," Binky announced into Lexi's ear when she picked up the telephone. "Want to come along?"

Lexi glanced at her watch. There was plenty of time to do her chores later. "Sure."

"Great! Meet us at the toy store in the mall in half an hour. Okay?"

"I'll be there."

Lexi was thoughtful as she hung up the phone. Binky and Nicole spent a lot of time at the mall on Saturdays. It seemed that Nicole had rarely had the opportunity before to wander the wide aisles and look at the things most children enjoyed and took for granted. Binky had told Lexi that Nicole's main pleasure was the children's section at the library and her second was watching the water fountains at the mall.

Lexi jotted a quick note to her mother and headed for the door.

They were exactly where Binky had said they would be—directly in front of the toy store, gazing at a display of singing daisies. Nicole was laughing and clapping her hands. When Lexi approached them, Nicole reached out and grabbed her hand.

"Look, Lexi! Aren't they funny? Binky says they're transistor radios with little mechanical flowers on top!"

Lexi was less struck by the singing flowers than she was by the fact that Nicole had reached out and touched her. The child had changed considerably in the past few weeks. Binky was definitely bringing out the best in Nicole. She was more friendly and outgoing each time Lexi saw her.

"Want to look around inside?" Binky asked. "They must have some new displays in here by now."

Nicole nodded eagerly. "I wish I had some money. I'd buy that stuffed rabbit. He'd look so cute on my window seat, wouldn't he, Binky?"

"You'd better start saving your money," Binky said with a smile. "I've been hearing about that rabbit for days!"

The threesome walked into the store and Nicole led them to the stuffed toy section.

"Oh! It's on sale!" Nicole stared longingly at a gangly rabbit with huge floppy feet and long ears. She dug in her pockets. "And I still don't have enough money."

Binky glanced at Lexi. She could see the affection and caring in Binky's eyes. "Maybe I could give you some, Nicole."

Nicole turned huge eyes toward Binky. "You'd do that?"

"Sure. If I have enough. I'm not very good at saving my money."

Nicole's face fell. "I couldn't take it. Then you wouldn't have any left."

Binky pulled some wrinkled bills out of her pocket. "That's okay. I just bought some new clothes with my first paycheck. I don't need anything right now. Here—take this." She thrust the money into Nicole's hands. The child looked startled and unsure of herself.

"Take it," Binky insisted. "What are friends for?"

The little girl beamed. "You're doing this because you're my friend?"

"Of course! Now, go and buy it before someone else does."

"I'll pay you back. I promise I will!" Nicole darted off with a huge smile on her face.

"That was nice of you," Lexi smiled.

"She's been wanting that rabbit for a long time," Binky explained. "It's worth it just to see her smile."

"She's very serious, isn't she?"

"*Too* serious, I think. But, I'm working on it. I'm trying to gain her trust. Then she might relax and start being happy like a little kid should be."

Binky and Lexi didn't have time to finish the conversation. Nicole came dashing back with the big rabbit in her arms, the sales receipt stapled to one ear.

"They said I could carry him without a bag. Isn't he beautiful?"

The older girls admired the floppy-eared toy almost as much as Nicole as they walked toward the fountain at the center of the mall. They were only a few steps from their destination when a gruff voice called out to them.

"Hey! Where'd you get that dumb-looking rabbit?"

Four boys, all about fourteen or fifteen years old, were leaning against the railing that rimmed the fountain. All were sneering at Nicole and the rabbit.

"Dumbest looking thing I've ever seen," one commented. He was over six feet tall and had dark, uncombed hair.

"Yeah. Almost as dumb-looking as the kid who's carrying it!" The boy who spoke wore a sweatshirt with the sleeves torn off raggedly at the shoulders.

"No lie. Hey, kid! Is that your pet or your twin sister?" he laughed jeeringly.

Lexi could see Nicole shrinking under the cruel jibes. Just as she reached to grab Nicole's hand, she heard another angry voice.

"Who do you think you're calling dumb?" Binky—all one hundred pounds of her—was standing in front of the boys. Her hands were on her hips and her head was erect, her eyes defiant.

"Who's this squirt?" the tall one asked.

"And who's the childish one?" Binky retorted. The big boy looked startled.

Lexi held back a giggle. The whole scene reminded her of the David and Goliath story. It seemed as though the tiny Binky was before a giant, defending her own.

"You guys must have something better to do than taunt a little kid. What else do you do for fun? Kick crutches out from under little old ladies? Pull the wings off butterflies? Grow up!"

The young boys stared at Binky dumbfounded.

She continued. "I think you should apologize to this child. She bought that toy with her own money. You have no right to make fun of her or frighten her."

"Heck! I'm sorry! You don't have to get so huffy!" The boy with the ragged sleeves was blushing a bright pink. Binky had gathered a crowd.

"And you don't have to act like a jerk!" She spun around on her heel. "Come on, Nicole. Let's get out of here." She towed the little girl into the nearest store, and Lexi hurried to follow.

"Good for you!" Lexi cheered once they were out of hearing distance. "You were great!"

"They just made me so mad, Lexi. Nicole, are you okay, honey? Just forget about those mean boys. I don't know what their problem was!"

Nicole stared at Binky intently. Finally, she spoke.

"You really like me, don't you, Binky?"

"Of course I do!"

"I mean *really* like me!"

"I *really* like you, Nicole."

A tear sprang from Nicole's eye. She reached up and wiped it away.

"You're my first real friend," she said seriously.

Binky glanced at Lexi, who had moved discreetly away. "Thank you, honey, but I'm sure you've had lots of friends."

"No, I haven't. None. I have to go to the restaurant after school. I can't have other girls over to play with me, ever."

"Oh, I see, but—"

"You are, Binky. You're my first real friend."

Binky tried to conceal her surprise. "Well, thanks. I guess I'm pretty lucky—now I have *two* best friends!"

Nicole looked at Lexi. "Is she your friend?"

Binky nodded. "That's right. Lexi and you are my best friends." She glanced around. "Let's get something to drink," she suggested.

Once they were situated in a booth in the Food Pavilion, Nicole continued the conversation where they'd left off. "What do best friends do, Binky?"

The question was so innocent and so sincere that it made Lexi feel like crying. Poor kid! She didn't even know what it was like to have a best friend!

"Well, we spend time together and we study together and we tell each other secrets."

"What kinds of secrets?" Nicole wondered.

Lexi laughed. "Things about ourselves. Embarrassing things that have happened to us that we wouldn't tell another person in the whole world."

"And things we think about," Binky continued. "It's hard to explain, really. Friends just know each other very, very well."

"Friends can tell each other *anything* and still be friends?" Nicole wondered. She seemed fascinated by the conversation.

"That's right."

"Anything?" Nicole looked amazed.

Binky nodded, looking very serious.

Nicole made no further comment. Instead, she took a long, thirsty sip of her soda.

Chapter Nine

"Am I late?" Lexi asked as she came hurrying into the Hamburger Shack. Todd, Harry and Binky were already sitting at one of their favorite tables. Todd and Harry had double cheeseburgers and stacks of french fries in front of them. Binky was twirling a straw in a small soda.

"No," Todd said with a smile. "Harry and I were here first and we ordered. Binky just came. What would you like to eat?"

Lexi looked at the huge stack of french fries and at Binky's small drink. "Are you eating anything, Binky?" she asked.

Binky shook her head.

"Maybe I'll just have a burger," Lexi said. "No onions." Todd nodded and went to the counter to place her order. Lexi slid into the seat next to his, swiping a french fry on the way by his plate.

"Jennifer and I are working on a new piece of music," she explained. "Mrs. Waverly offered to help us this afternoon. I didn't expect to take so long."

"Burger's on its way," Todd said as he returned

to the table. "I ordered you a shake, just in case."

"And what if I don't want it?" Lexi replied with a grin.

"I guess I'll just have to suffer and drink it for you. Now that's true friendship, huh?"

"Yeah," Harry put in. "Maybe you should have ordered a banana split, too—just in case she wanted one. I could have helped you with that."

The boys bantered back and forth across the table, but Lexi noticed that Binky did not join in. It was as though she wasn't even hearing what was going on around her.

"What's new?" Lexi asked, keeping one eye on Binky.

"Harry's been telling us some stories about work," Todd said. "Sounds as though you really have to be on your toes if you work for the Marlinis."

"Oh?" Lexi looked from Binky to Harry. "Why do you say that?"

Harry shrugged nonchalantly. "Well, for starters, Mr. Marlini fired two people today. I guess he's fired lots of them, but these are the first two that I've seen go."

"What could they have done?" Lexi wondered. "It must have been something pretty serious."

Harry shrugged again. "Well, maybe. I didn't see it that way. Butch and Jamie were supposed to be in charge of the salad bar. They're prep cooks. The salad bar at The Willows is about a half-mile long. And of course, Mr. Marlini thinks it has to be perfect. There are supposed to be forty-five different selections, and each one has its spot. Beginning with lettuce, endive and spinach, you build your salad all the way up to sunflower seeds, hot peppers and bacon bits."

"Makes sense to me," Todd interjected through a mouthful of french fries.

"Well, Butch and Jamie started getting a little careless. They put grated cheese where the onions should go and green peppers into the sliced mushroom slot, not thinking it was any big deal. The salad bar looked fine to me, but when Mr. Marlini came to check it, he was furious."

"He hauled this big chart from the kitchen that had the salad bar mapped out with every spot labeled. He screamed and yelled and pointed out the spots where the cheese and green peppers should have been, waving his hands in Butch and Jamie's faces." Harry looked serious. "His face got all red. I wondered for a minute if he'd have a heart attack or something."

"All over misplaced cheese and peppers?" Lexi asked in amazement.

Harry nodded. "That's what I mean. It didn't seem like such a big deal to me. What customer would possibly notice the difference? I don't think any of them have it memorized anyway."

"And he fired the two guys for that?" Todd whistled. "He is tough."

"Some people are very strict and have high expectations. I imagine Mr. Marlini couldn't have gotten where he is now by being careless or sloppy," Lexi said. She was trying to justify Mr. Marlini's behavior, but still, it did seem very strange to become so upset over such a little matter.

"He's successful, all right. Successful—but hated."

"Who hates him?" Todd asked.

"Most everyone who works for him." Harry glanced at Binky before continuing. "I'm finding that out. I don't, but I've never gotten into trouble. I'm very, very careful not to make him angry. When Mr. Marlini chews someone out, it makes me plenty nervous."

Just then, Binky gave an agitated little wave of her hand and knocked over her soda. The sticky liquid spread across the table. "Oh no!" she squeaked.

"Someone grab a towel," Harry said, as Lexi began tossing napkins over the puddle.

Todd dashed to the counter for something to mop up the mess.

"Oh, I'm sorry. I didn't mean to—I don't know what happened. I guess I just didn't realize that Mr. Marlini was like that. What a mess!" Binky babbled on, looking very distressed. Todd, Harry and Lexi were all surprised at her unusual behavior.

"It's just a soda, Binky," Harry stated calmly. "I'll buy you another one."

"No." Binky held up her hand and shook her head repeatedly. "I don't want another one. I'd like to go home."

"Did you get some on your clothes?" Lexi asked.

"No, no. I just want to go home."

Lexi glanced at Harry. He was looking as confused as she. "But we just got here, Binky."

Binky looked agitated. "I know and I'm sorry. You guys can stay. I just really need to be going home." She pushed herself away from the table and began to leave.

"Wait up," Todd called after her. "Let Harry and

me finish our food and we'll take you home."

Binky looked unsure for a moment, then nodded. "I suppose so. But I really want to go right home."

The boys hurriedly finished. When Lexi's hamburger came, she downed it quickly, and without further conversation they were out the door within ten minutes.

"Wait here and I'll bring the car around," Todd instructed as he loped off to the parking lot.

Harry turned to Binky. "Are you sure you're all right?" His eyes were dark with concern. "I mean, are you sick or something?"

When Binky shook her head mutely, Harry turned to Lexi, who shrugged her shoulders. She didn't understand what was happening any more than the boys did.

Todd pulled up in his Ford coupe and beeped the horn twice. "Your ride is here," he said with a grin.

Harry opened the door, ushered Binky into the backseat and climbed in after her. Lexi slid in beside Todd. He gave her a sharp glance and mouthed the question, "What's wrong?"

Lexi shrugged. "I wish I knew," she said softly.

The ride to the McNaughton house was in continued silence. Todd had barely come to a stop when Binky scrambled over Harry's lap to get to the door.

"Let me out, please," she said.

Lexi could hear a note of panic in her voice. "Are you sure you're going to be all right, Binky?" she asked.

Binky turned to her friend with very troubled eyes. "Lexi, could you come inside with me? Please?"

Lexi glanced at Todd and Harry and nodded.

"Sure. I'll be glad to. What about the guys?"

Binky shrugged nervously. "Umm. I don't know," she stammered.

"Listen. We've got things we need to do. Harry can come to my brother Mike's garage and help me work on the car." Todd patted the dashboard. "I think we should do that right now. Don't you, Harry?"

Harry nodded, anxious to leave the awkward situation. "Call you later," Todd said to Lexi.

Lexi paused to wave goodbye to the boys while Binky hurried up the steps to her door. Lexi followed.

Binky remained morose as she mounted the steps to her own bedroom. She flung herself across the bed. Lexi shut the door and punched in the lock.

"All right, Binky. Enough of this. Please tell me what's wrong," Lexi pleaded.

"I don't know," Binky said in a muffled voice. The lower portion of her face was buried in her pillow and her eyes were round and troubled as she stared at Lexi. "I really don't know."

"First you won't eat anything at the Hamburger Shack," Lexi said; "then you won't speak to us, and then suddenly you spill your drink and jump up, insisting you have to go home, and you still say you don't know what's wrong?"

"I'm sorry about the Hamburger Shack. I was just upset."

"And what were you upset about?" Lexi used her softest, most empathizing tone.

"I can't explain it." Binky buried her face in her pillow and rolled onto her back. "Never mind."

"It's too late for that," Lexi insisted. "I *do* mind. I mind that I practically had to swallow my hamburger whole. I mind that we didn't have any fun with Todd and Harry. I mind most of all that one of my very best friends in the entire world is terribly upset."

Impulsively, Lexi stated, "You're upset about what Harry was saying about Mr. Marlini firing those boys, aren't you?"

Binky's thin shoulders moved slightly.

"Maybe you weren't upset about them, but you were upset with Mr. Marlini." Lexi sensed she was on the right track. "It wasn't even Mr. Marlini. Actually, it's Nicole, isn't it?"

Binky withdrew the pillow from her face and stared at Lexi. She nodded slowly and somberly. "I don't know what to do about Nicole, Lexi. I've never met another child like her."

"In what way?" Lexi queried. "You know her better than I do by now."

"She's so serious and so intense. And so, so old."

"Old?" Lexi echoed. "What do you mean by that?"

"I don't know, really," Binky said honestly. "It's just that she's a *very* unhappy child. I'm really, really worried about her."

A frown creased Lexi's forehead. "Why would you worry about Nicole? She has a beautiful home and clothes and her parents are well off. There are kids much less fortunate to worry about."

"I know that," Binky said. "But there's more to this than you see at first. Trust me."

"You'll have to explain that to me."

"It's like she's been hurt, Lexi."

"Hurt?" Lexi said incredulously. "Like, in physically hurt?"

"No. Not really. More like afraid."

Lexi looked at Binky for a long moment. Binky's face was more pinched than usual, and she didn't look much older than Nicole herself.

"What do you think she's afraid of, Binky?"

Binky sat cross-legged on her bed. She tucked her toes under her knees and rocked back and forth as if that would bring the answer.

"I've been asking that myself. Nicole doesn't talk very much, you know, so all I can do is guess at what's bothering her."

"So? What do you think?"

Binky was about to answer, and then shook her head. "No. It's too crazy, really."

"What do you mean; who do you think Nicole is afraid of?" Lexi persisted.

Binky sighed, "Well, it's pretty weird, Lexi, but I really think Nicole is afraid of her own parents."

"Huh?" Lexi said blankly. "Her parents?"

Binky nodded. "Her dad, especially. When Harry was talking about him tonight and how he got angry and fired people for mixing up the salad bar, it just made me think about Nicole. I didn't mean to get upset and ruin the evening, but I couldn't help it. She's so innocent and so vulnerable. Every day I know her, she scares me even more. She's pretty and she's perfectly groomed, and she has everything she could want. Yet, she acts so timid and afraid. The only people I can imagine that she's afraid of are her parents." Binky's brave face crumpled. "I wish I hadn't heard Harry talk about Mr. Marlini. Maybe I never would have thought these things."

Lexi had a weak, sick feeling in her stomach.

"You were thinking these things before Harry mentioned Mr. Marlini, weren't you, Binky?"

Binky looked downcast. She nodded slowly. "I guess I was. Hearing Harry talk about Nicole's father made me realize what I had been thinking all along."

Now it was Lexi's turn to be upset. Silently she sank onto the corner of Binky's bed.

"Lexi?" Binky asked. "Now you look worried. Are you all right?"

"Not really," Lexi said in a faint voice. "This conversation reminds me of something that I've tried to forget."

Binky moved to her friend's side. "Tell me about it."

Lexi shrugged weakly. "It's just that this whole situation sounds familiar to me."

"Familiar? In what way?"

"When I was younger," Lexi began, "I had a good friend in Grover's Point. Her name was Laura." She stared out the window as she continued her story. "She was a lot like Nicole, now that I think about it. Laura had huge green eyes and lots of light blond hair with soft curls. She was just beautiful. She always looked as if she had come out of a store window. The only thing that could have made Laura prettier was a smile."

"She was like Nicole? She didn't smile much either?"

"Never. I remember my mom commenting on it once. Mom said Laura looked as though she were carrying the weight of the world on her thin little shoulders."

"So? Whatever happened to her? Have you heard about her since you moved out of Grover's Point?"

Lexi shook her head. "No. They moved away a long time before we did. Actually, Laura and her mother moved away one year and her dad moved the next."

"Why didn't they move together?" Binky didn't get it.

Lexi looked intently at her friend. "Laura was an abused child, Binky."

Binky looked surprised. "What do you mean by that?"

"Laura's dad was having a hard time with his business. The way my mom and dad explained it, he was very frustrated and he didn't have anyone he could talk to or anyone he could go to for help. He didn't go to a church and he would never let anyone get very close to him. So when he got upset, he really had nowhere to turn, so sometimes he'd take it out on Laura."

Binky's eyes were wide and her mouth dropped open in a relaxed gasp. "You mean, he hit her?"

"Sometimes," Lexi said softly. "Sometimes he'd just speak to her in offensive or degrading language. No matter what Laura did, she could never please him. I remember when she'd take home papers from school with really good grades and he'd say things like, 'Well, now I suppose you think you're really smart.' But, if she *didn't* bring home a decent grade, he'd tell her that she was stupid and that he was ashamed she was his daughter. No matter what she tried, Laura could never please him."

"But why would he do that to his own daughter?" Binky wondered.

"My mom said it was because Laura's father thought that kind of treatment would make her work harder and be better at what she did—kind of make up for his own failure."

Binky wrinkled her nose. "It wouldn't make me work harder."

"Of course not," Lexi agreed. "My mother told me later that emotional abuse like that could be just as harmful as physical abuse or neglect."

"Once, when he was really upset, he locked her in the basement and left her there in the dark. Laura tried to come up the steps and fell and broke her leg. That's when they discovered what had been going on."

"I don't understand," Binky protested. "Why didn't she complain?"

"She was afraid," Lexi said simply.

"I'd tell someone! I wouldn't let anybody hurt me!" Binky was adamant.

"I think she was afraid of being taken away from her mother and dad," Lexi reasoned.

Binky looked thoughtful. "Oh, I never thought of that. I suppose that would be pretty scary, too," she admitted.

"My mom told me that not many people realize that parents who hurt their children can be helped. There are counselors and social workers and doctors—all kinds of people who want to help kids stay with their parents and have normal lives. I know that's all Laura really wanted—just a normal life. A dad who would treat her better."

"You know, I never thought about emotional child abuse," Binky admitted. "I always thought it had to be something physical or—" She flushed. "You know, sexual."

"The way my parents explained it to me is that emotional abuse can be just as bad as physical or sexual abuse if it prevents a child from growing up normally. Mom said that a lot of times abuse is a mixture of all three kinds—sexual, emotional and physical."

"How terrible." Binky looked as if she was ready to cry. "Poor little girl. Whatever happened to her?"

"I don't really know," Lexi admitted. "Laura's mother took her away. She got a divorce from Laura's father and I never heard about them again."

Both girls were silent for a long while, contemplating the nightmare of Laura's life. Then Lexi asked cautiously, "Do you think that could be Nicole's problem?"

Binky turned to her in disbelief. She shook her head. "Oh no. It can't be. That's just too awful. I'm sure that Nicole's father isn't hitting her. Mr. Marlini wouldn't do that." There was a long pause. The air seemed thick with emotion. Binky dropped her eyes to the floor and she added in a very small voice, "Besides, I already looked for bruises."

The sick feeling grew in the pit of Lexi's stomach.

"You don't have to hide anything from me, Binky. You can say what you actually think."

The pain on Binky's face was heart-wrenching to see. "I've been having all these awful thoughts about Nicole's parents, Lexi. What business is it of mine? Maybe the kid is just strange. Maybe she's just scared and timid by nature and will grow out of it. What can I really do about it?"

"It's always your business if someone's being hurt and you can help them," Lexi said sternly. "Have you ever heard the parable of the good Samaritan?"

"Oh, yeah," Binky mused. "Isn't it about the guy who found someone beaten up along the roadside and picked him up and took him to an inn for care until he was well?"

Lexi nodded. "That's it; but others passed by that man lying in the ditch before the good Samaritan came along. There was only one man who acted like Jesus would have us act. There was only one man who took the time to stop to help the one in trouble."

"Oh." Binky's voice was small and weak. "Are you telling me that I have to be a good Samaritan?"

Lexi nodded soberly. "It's hard, I know."

"But you're the good Christian, Lexi," Binky wailed. "Maybe it means that people like you should help."

"But I'm not the one in this situation," Lexi reasoned. "Besides, helping is always the right thing to do."

"This Christianity stuff of yours isn't easy, is it?" Binky said with a sigh.

"No one ever said it would be, but there are a lot of rewards in it."

"If you say so. Still," and Binky frowned, "sometimes I'm not so sure about this Jesus stuff. Like right now. I'm not so sure that my over-active imagination didn't make up all this stuff about Nicole and her dad. Why, I bet if we went over there right now, they'd be laughing and playing games and having a great time and I'd feel like a real fool."

That thought seemed to cheer Binky. "That's it.

I'd feel really dumb, Lexi. I've been imagining all sorts of awful things and I could be all wrong. Mr. Marlini is really a nice man. He'd never do anything like that to his daughter. Besides," she concluded, "Nicole and I were playing in the water sprinklers yesterday, and even in her bathing suit, I couldn't detect a single black and blue mark, not even on her knees. When I was growing up, I always had bruised knees. I must be wrong, Lexi. I'm sure I am. Let's just forget the whole idea."

Binky obviously wanted to forget this conversation, but Lexi persisted. "There are other ways to abuse children, Binky. Like I just told you—emotionally."

"I think you're letting your imagination get the best of you," Binky insisted. "Maybe because of your friend Laura and her experience. Just because Mr. Marlini is strict and Nicole respects him, that doesn't mean he's hurting her."

"True," Lexi agreed. "But the way you've been talking, there's got to be something more."

"I think I'm making trouble where there isn't any, Lexi," Binky decided. Her voice was firm. "I don't want to talk about this anymore." Her chin stuck out stubbornly. "Besides, Mr. Marlini is so rich and so smart! What could make him do anything as awful as that? Then her face crumpled. "Oh, Lexi, what do I do? What can I do to help Nicole? What if there really *is* something wrong?"

Chapter Ten

Lexi chewed thoughtfully on her lower lip. "I guess the most important thing, Binky, is to be sure that something is actually wrong. Then, if Nicole really is in trouble, you need to find someone to help her."

Binky's slim body hunched into a worried slump. "I really hope I'm just imagining this, Lexi. Every family's different. How did I get into thinking such awful things about Nicole's parents?" Binky's look hardened. "Maybe I deserve to be fired. Just like those guys at the restaurant."

Lexi sighed and patted her friend's arm comfortingly. "I think I'll go home and ask for some help. You're going to need it."

Binky nodded, knowing exactly how Lexi's mind worked in problem situations. "You're going to pray, aren't you?"

"I think it's a good time for it."

"Maybe so," Binky said with a sigh. "I know this is bigger than I am."

As Lexi walked down the street toward her own

home, she thought of Binky's last words. "This is bigger than I am." So many things were just that— bigger than she or any other human being could understand or solve alone. That's what made it so wonderful to have a loving Father who was greater and wiser than anything or anyone on the face of the earth.

It was comforting for Lexi to know that she could tap into power like that and ask for help in any situation—including the one in which Binky and Nicole now found themselves.

The Leighton house was quiet. Lexi could hear her mother and Ben talking softly in the kitchen. Silently, she tiptoed to her room to get her Bible.

Because she didn't have a particular verse in mind, Lexi put the Bible on her lap and paged through it. She scanned the pages in search of some words to calm her worried heart.

Luke 18:16 stood out on the page. "Let the children come to me, and do not hinder them; for to such belongs the kingdom of God."

Lexi curled up comfortably on her bed and nestled into the pillows. Suddenly what had been troubling her was becoming very clear. Jesus wants the little children near to Him. Jesus loves them. He doesn't want anything to stand in the way of their coming into His kingdom. The verse made it so clear. God *does* care about children and what happens to them—Nicole Marlini in particular. Lexi was more sure than ever that Binky needed to discover what was going on in the child's life.

"Lexi? Are you home?" Mrs. Leighton mounted the stairs.

"In here, Mom." Gently, she replaced the Bible on her nightstand.

"Are you alone? I wasn't sure if you'd come in. I hope I didn't interrupt anything, Lexi."

"That's okay, Mom. I was just thinking."

"About what, dear?"

"Mom, have you ever known a child abuser?"

Mrs. Leighton appeared surprised at her question. "Hmm, someone who mistreats children? Why do you ask?"

"I guess I'm just wondering what they're like."

"Well, if you mean are they big, ugly, or mean looking, they aren't. It's not always easy to identify such a person."

Lexi nodded. "I guess that's what I wondered."

Mrs. Leighton continued. "We've probably all known someone who has abused a child, but we don't realize it."

"Why is that, Mom?" Lexi asked.

"I'm not an expert, Lexi, but from what reading I've done, it is known that child abusers come from every occupation and level of society, any age or color. It can be a man or a woman, rich or poor. Unfortunately, some may even profess a religious faith, while others may have no belief in God at all."

"So, you're saying anyone could be guilty of child abuse?"

Mrs. Leighton nodded. "I'll tell you why I think that's true, Lexi."

Lexi was listening intently.

"We don't always understand people's own life experiences. People who abuse others were often abused themselves as children. They've learned wrong ways of relating to children from their own parents."

"That doesn't make sense to me," Lexi responded. "If you were beaten or hurt in any way as a child, why would you want to hurt your own kids?"

"It's because of their own warped experience. They think the way they were treated is the normal way people treat children. Sadly, that idea is often handed down from generation to generation." Mrs. Leighton looked out the window for a moment before she spoke again. Her voice was sad and melancholic. "I went to school with a boy whose father abused his sister."

"You did, Mom?" Lexi gasped. "How awful!"

"Well, it's not the sort of thing you enjoy talking about, Lexi, but since you're wondering about identifying such a situation—this one was very complex. My friend actually related the problem to me some years later. It seemed that his father never experienced much love from his own parents when he was a child. He really didn't know how to express affection to his own children. He didn't hurt the others, only his daughter. There seemed to be bad chemistry between them."

"Bad chemistry?" Lexi echoed. "What do you mean by that, Mom?"

"Well, for one thing, his daughter looked very much like the man's own mother, who had abused *him* when he was growing up. No matter what that child did, as innocent as she was, her father associated her with the beatings his own mother had given him."

"I guess I can understand that," Lexi murmured.

"When he fathered a daughter that looked like his mother, he took out his frustrations and pent-up anger on her."

"Where was the little girl's mother?" Lexi asked indignantly.

"Caught right in the middle, as far as I could tell," Mrs. Leighton said. "She was being forced to choose between her husband and her child. Rather than face what was happening in her family, she tried to ignore it. In fact, she made up such logical excuses for the bruises and tears that it was many years before anyone learned what her husband had done."

"Are all child abusers like that?" Lexi asked.

"Oh no. Everyone is different. Each person has his own set of emotional baggage to carry—his own extremely low self-esteem, his own hurts and anger, each stemming from different circumstances." Mrs. Leighton studied her daughter. "Why are you asking about this, Lexi?"

"Oh, Binky and I were talking about it today, Mom," Lexi replied honestly. She didn't want to mention Nicole Marlini until Binky had done further detective work and thought more thoroughly about her accusation.

"Well, you girls certainly talk about some heavy subjects," Mrs. Leighton said with a sigh.

"Too heavy," Lexi agreed.

"Remember, honey, if you ever have any other questions, you can always ask me."

They were abruptly interrupted with Ben's "I want to play!" He was standing in the doorway with his hands on his hips and a demanding expression on his face. "Lexi, play!" He spoke so emphatically that both Lexi and her mother burst out laughing.

Lexi jumped up from the bed. "I'd love to play with you, Ben. Come on, let's go find a game."

Lexi really was eager to play with her little brother. She wanted to forget about the subject she and her mother had discussed, and more particularly the problem closer to home, which involved Nicole.

After dinner Binky called Lexi.

"How are things going?" Lexi was eager to know. "Better, I hope."

Binky sounded distant and sad. "I don't know. Not really."

"Oh?" Lexi murmured. "What's been happening?"

"I've been really listening and watching today, Lexi. Maybe too hard. Maybe I'm reading trouble into common, ordinary activities."

"Tell me, Binky" Lexi insisted. "What things have you noticed?"

"Well, today Nicole told me that her parents really wanted a baby boy when she was born."

Lexi thought for a minute. "Well, I guess that's not so unusual. Most parents have a preference. But they also are actually happy with either sex when the child is born."

"True," Binky agreed. "But in Nicole's case, they weren't happy, because they keep reminding her that they wanted a boy. And she's nine years old!"

"Oh. What else did Nicole say?" Lexi asked.

Binky's voice wavered. "She said that sometimes when her dad gets angry with her, he tells her he wishes she'd never been born."

"Oh, how awful! What a horrible thing to hear from your own father!"

"And she told me that sometimes when she's been bad and Mr. Marlini is very upset with her, he punishes her by locking her in a closet."

Lexi gasped. "He locks her in a closet?"

"That's what she said, Lexi, and I believe her. She doesn't make things up. This child has no fantasy life at all. She's not allowed to watch television, and even if she had read about something like this, I don't think a nine-year-old would say anything like that unless it was true."

Lexi's hand was suddenly trembling as she held the telephone. "I'm scared, Binky."

"I know. Me too. I'm scared for Nicole." Then Binky added, "Actually, I'm scared for myself. Now what do I do?"

"Well, we're just kids," Lexi said. "We can't do anything by ourselves. We have to tell someone."

"But who?" Binky pleaded.

"Binky, do you remember when Jennifer was being so rebellious in school and cut her hair crazy and everything?"

"Sure," Binky replied. "How could I forget? They discovered she had dyslexia and was rebelling because she was so frustrated."

"It was Todd's mom that helped her. She was the one who first figured out Jennifer's problem. She's the coordinator for the handicapped learning programs in the county. Maybe she knows something about child abuse. At least she could tell us what we need to do next. Would you mind if I talked to Todd and his mom about this, Binky?"

Lexi could hear the relief in Binky's voice, "Of course not. I don't want to be alone in this, Lexi. I know I can't handle it. But, what's going to happen to Nicole if her dad finds out that she told on him, Lexi? What will happen then?"

"I don't know the answer to that, Binky, but I know that we have to do something. Let me call Mrs. Winston. I'll get back to you."

"Thanks, Lexi; you're a real friend."

As Lexi hung up the phone, she felt unsure. She murmured a prayer asking for wisdom and strength as she dialed the Winstons' number. Much to Lexi's relief, it was Todd who answered the phone.

"Winston residence. Todd speaking."

"Todd, this is Lexi."

"Hi, Lex. What's happening?"

"I need to talk to someone."

"Well, Todd's ear is always here," he said with a chuckle. "What do you want to talk about?"

"It's hard to talk about on the phone."

"Well, come on over. Do you need a ride?"

"No, that's okay. I'll bike."

"I'll be here all evening," Todd said cheerfully. "Come right now, if you want."

Lexi called to her mother to tell her where she'd be and was on her bike pedaling down the street in a matter of minutes. When she coasted into the Winston driveway, Lexi was relieved to see Mrs. Winston's car.

Todd was standing in the garage doorway, examining his car's tires. "Hi, Lexi. That was fast. Come on inside."

Mrs. Winston was in the kitchen clearing up the

last of the evening meal. She looked crisp and pretty as usual, even with an apron covering her red business suit.

"Hello, Lexi. It's nice to see you. Todd, there's pie left if you and Lexi would like to have some with a glass of milk. I'll leave you two alone."

"Mrs. Winston?" Lexi blurted out before she lost her nerve. "Would you mind staying for a few minutes?"

Todd and his mother both looked surprised. "Not at all, dear. What is it?"

"Well, I need some advice. Probably some help, actually."

Mrs. Winston settled herself on a stool at the counter, concern on her face. "Is something troubling you, Lexi? You look worried."

Todd stood beside Lexi, his arm around her shoulders. "Lex? You can tell us anything. What's wrong?"

"It's not for me, ex-exactly," Lexi stammered, at a loss for words. "It's for Binky. Well, not Binky either, but for someone who's very close to Binky."

This wasn't easy, Lexi decided. She was beginning to wish that she'd never gotten into this. She thought of how ostriches have the right idea—sticking their heads into the sand when trouble's around. At least they couldn't see it.

Mrs. Winston put her hands on Lexi's. "Start from the beginning."

Lexi drew a deep breath and plunged into her story. She explained first how much Binky had wanted a job and how she had so easily been hired by the Marlinis to care for their daughter. Then Lexi described Nicole—her beautiful gray-green eyes, her dark blond curls, and her shy, quiet ways. Then, her voice shaking, Lexi told Todd and Mrs. Winston that Binky suspected Nicole was being abused. When she relayed the incident about Nicole being locked in a closet, Mrs. Winston's grim look turned to anger.

"How perfectly dreadful!"

"Binky's scared, Mrs. Winston. We thought we should tell an adult who might know what to do. Could you help Binky?"

"Well, I certainly know people who can," Mrs. Winston said.

"I thought you might," Lexi murmured. "I remember how you helped Jennifer before she knew that she had dyslexia."

Mrs. Winston smiled softly at Lexi. "You're a very brave and caring girl, Lexi."

She dismissed the compliment with a shrug. "I want to help my friend. She's worried that she'll get into trouble for telling anyone these things, Mrs. Winston. She's afraid of what Mr. Marlini might say, particularly if it's all a big mistake."

Mrs. Winston patted Lexi's hand. "Lexi, if Nicole is being abused, there's no doubt in my mind that you're doing the right thing. I do understand what Binky's going through. Reporting something like this can be very, very frightening. Besides that, you're unsure if anyone will believe you. But, if you're certain that a person is being abused, you really must report it. It's not the kind of problem you can solve on your own. The most important thing is that Binky is certain of the facts. I'd like to speak with her myself so I can hear exactly what Nicole told her before we call anyone. It would be dreadful if this were all a mistake."

"Binky's afraid for Nicole, too, that she might get into trouble for talking. She's never had to deal with anything like this before."

"Let me talk to Binky, Lexi. Don't worry about it now. You did the right thing. You came to an adult who can help you with your problem. If, after talking to Binky, I think there's a need, I'll help her to make up the report. Because of my position, I've had to deal with difficult things like this many times. I certainly want to help Binky get through it."

Todd had been sitting quietly the entire time Lexi and his mother were talking. Now he asked a question that made Lexi's stomach lurch and dip as if she were riding on a roller coaster. "Will they take Nicole away from her parents?" he asked.

What had she and Binky gotten themselves into? Lexi's mind raced through all the consequences. Perhaps it would be better to look away, to pretend that nothing had happened, than to risk the possibility of breaking up the family

"No, Todd, that's not always the case," Mrs. Winston answered simply. "If the family agrees to go for counseling, that would not be necessary. There are lots of ways that parents can get help nowadays. There are parent groups, hotlines, and therapists available for special counsel."

Mrs. Winston leaned over and gave Lexi a hug. "Don't worry now, honey. You did the right thing by coming to me."

Lexi looked at them both a moment before speaking. "Thank you so much, Mrs. Winston. I'd better go home now."

"Do you want me to walk you?" Todd asked, concern in his voice.

Lexi shook her head. "It's all right, Todd. I'd like to be alone for a while if you don't mind."

Todd nodded, his eyes full of understanding. "You call me when you need me, all right?" he said.

Todd walked her to the front door of the house and gave her shoulders a squeeze. "I'll be here for you, Lex. Anytime."

With those comforting words, Lexi biked toward home to do the one thing she could for Nicole and Binky and this dreadful situation. She was going to pray.

Chapter Eleven

It was after ten o'clock when Binky finally returned Lexi's call. "Where have you been, Bink?" Lexi wondered. "I've been trying to reach you for over two hours."

"I was just out walking," Binky admitted. Her voice sounded mechanical and distant.

"Binky? Has anything else happened?"

"No. I'm just scared, Lexi. *Really* scared."

"Of course you are. I know that," Lexi said. "But everything is going to be okay. I talked to Mrs. Winston and she said—"

"I want to back out, Lexi. Please, I don't want her to tell anyone."

"What?" Lexi blurted. "I thought we decided it was best to tell someone."

"I know what we decided," Binky said. "But now I'm *undecided*. I don't want Mrs. Winston to check into this stuff with the Marlinis. I think I must be wrong. My imagination has gotten the best of me. I've probably been watching too much television and dreamed all this up."

126

Now what? Lexi thought. Could they turn their backs on this situation so easily? She doubted that very much. They'd come too far. But how was she going to convince Binky otherwise? *Oh, help, Father,* Lexi petitioned.

"There's nothing you can say that will make me change my mind," Binky continued firmly. "Nothing at all. I've made a mistake and I don't want to make things any worse."

"Hang on, Binky. I want to read something to you—something I discovered last night."

Before Binky could respond, Lexi laid down the phone and ran to her room for her Bible. When she returned to the phone, she could hear Binky humming impatiently on the other end of the line. "I was reading my Bible last night, Binky, and I ran across some verses that I want you to hear."

"It's not going to help," Binky responded sourly. "You've always got verses for everything, but this time they won't work."

"Listen, I had Nicole on my mind last night when I was having my devotional time. And these verses stood out to me."

"So?" Binky said suspiciously. "What does that have to do with me?"

"Here it is, Bink. 'Let the children come to me, and do not hinder them, for to such belongs the kingdom of God. Truly, I say to you, whoever does not receive the kingdom of God like a child shall not enter it,'" Lexi read, quoting from Luke 18.

"Yeah. So?"

"Jesus loved the children, Binky. Listen to another verse from Matthew. 'Now they were bringing even infants to him that he might touch them; and when the disciples saw it, they rebuked them. But Jesus called them to him, saying, 'Let the children come to me, and do not hinder them; for to such belongs the kingdom of God.' In Mark 10 it says the same thing and adds: 'And he [Jesus] took them in his arms and blessed them, laying his hands upon them.' "

"Of course, Jesus loved children. Big deal. I think we could have figured that out, Lexi. You won't convince me to change my mind about this. I've been a busybody. I had no right to interfere."

"Don't you see what these verses are saying?" Lexi persisted. "First, that Jesus loves children and that none of us should ever prevent a child from coming to Him. But He's also saying something else."

"And you're going to tell me about it, right?" Binky said sarcastically.

"These passages are saying that anyone who trusts God like he'd trust his own father is part of God's kingdom."

"So?" Binky replied, not getting Lexi's point.

"Don't you see? Jesus is asking us to believe in Him as we might believe our own fathers. I love my dad and he loves me. He never lies to me or treats me badly. Neither does yours."

"True," Binky said resignedly.

"What kind of a message is Mr. Marlini giving Nicole? That fathers are good and kind and patient? Or that they're impatient and angry and sometimes punish too harshly? How can Nicole love a *heavenly* Father if she thinks He's like her *earthly* one?"

"Seems to me that's God's problem, not mine,"

Binky replied stubbornly. "I don't want to be involved. Listen, Lexi. I've got to go. I need to think. I'm so mixed up . . . I just don't know what to do. I don't want to cause any trouble, but I don't want anything to happen to Nicole, either."

Lexi said goodbye and hung up the phone thoughtfully. She hadn't meant to confuse Binky any more than she already was. The thought of Nicole Marlini and those haunting eyes had been tormenting her. If someone *were* hurting Nicole, it would have to stop. If someone *weren't* hurting her, then it was worth being embarrassed to be proven wrong.

The hours of the weekend seemed to stretch on unendingly. Each time the telephone rang Lexi hoped it was Binky, but Binky did not call. As always, when things were going wrong in her world, Lexi took comfort in her family.

Ben was delighted with every game Lexi played with him and every story she told. Saturday evening as Lexi and Ben were sitting on the front porch, Todd drove up.

"Hi. What's going on?" he greeted them.

"Eating watermelon." Ben smiled as wide as the slice he held in his hand. "See?"

"No kidding," Todd chuckled and ruffled Ben's silky brown hair. "I thought your face was always sticky like that."

"Maybe you should go inside and wash up now, Ben," Lexi said.

Ben looked down at the front of his shirt, which was stained with watermelon juice and covered with little black seeds. "Ben's a mess!" he announced. "Yuk." Obediently, he put down the watermelon rind, brushed the seeds onto the grass and went inside.

Lexi and Todd smiled at each other as the screen door slammed shut. "He's a good kid," Todd observed.

Lexi nodded. "One of the best. He's been keeping my mind occupied this weekend."

Todd nodded sympathetically. "I know what you mean. I've been working on my car at my brother's garage all day today. Seemed best to be out of the house."

"Have you heard anything?" Lexi wondered. "Has your mother said anything about Binky and the Marlinis?"

Todd shook his head. "Binky called Mom last night, but I don't know what the conversation was about. Mother won't say anything. I suppose it's none of our business, really."

"Maybe not, but I feel involved."

Todd nodded. "Mother said this is a very hard time for Binky."

"I've been praying for her, Todd. I really have."

He nodded briefly. "I guess that's about all we can do right now."

They sat together on the porch steps in companionable silence until dusk fell. Finally, Todd rose. "Well, I think I'd better go. I promised Jerry I'd meet him at the Hamburger Shack when he was finished with work."

"Say hi for me," Lexi said.

Jerry Randall was a lonely sort of boy who lived with his aunt and uncle while his parents worked for an oil company in the Persian Gulf. Jerry had had his ups and downs in the months that Lexi had known him, but now he seemed to be fairly happy and stable.

Lexi sighed. She had never realized how complicated life could be until she'd moved to Cedar River.

Perhaps it had something to do with growing older, she thought. Being *almost* an adult wasn't all it was cracked up to be.

———

By Sunday there was still no word from Binky. "You seem very restless today," Mrs. Leighton observed as Lexi wandered into the kitchen after church. "Why don't you make some lemonade?" Mrs. Leighton pushed a tray with a pitcher and a half dozen fresh lemons toward her.

It was nearly one o'clock when the doorbell rang. Lexi's heart skipped a beat when she saw Binky, Mrs. Winston and Todd standing outside.

"Come in," she said. "Is everything . . . I mean, what happened—are you okay, Binky?"

Binky nodded. Her small face seemed more pinched than ever, and her eyes were wide and serious.

"Binky wanted to talk to you, Lexi," Mrs. Winston explained. "May we sit down?"

"I made the report, Lexi," Binky said without preamble. "Mrs. Winston helped me."

Mrs. Winston slipped her arm around Binky's shoulder. "Binky did the right thing, Lexi. I've tried to assure her of that. It's very difficult to understand why parents would ever hurt their children."

"Why do they?" Lexi asked. "Why would an adult ever want to harm a child?"

Mrs. Winston's expression was thoughtful. "People who hurt their children usually don't have a very good opinion of themselves, Lexi. In many instances, these people feel like failures. They get it into their minds that they want their children to do better than their parents have done. Sometimes people have a tendency to push their children too hard, harder than children are able to tolerate."

"People just expect too much," Todd interjected.

"Children aren't little adults, and there are people who seem to forget this. Sometimes their expectations are much too high. When children don't do exactly as a parent wishes, the parent is disappointed or becomes angry."

"Do you think it's that way for the Marlinis?" Lexi asked, her expression puzzled. "Mr. Marlini is awfully successful. I don't see how Nicole could be a disappointment to him."

Mrs. Winston looked sad. "Well, Lexi, I can't say. Sometimes parents have simply put other things in their lives ahead of their children. Their work schedules, their careers. These people are normally under great pressure to succeed. Sometimes, this stress causes people to lash out at their children whether they mean to or not."

"Do you think Mr. Marlini is angry because things have gone wrong in his business and that's why he's taking it out on Nicole?"

Mrs. Winston shrugged. "I don't know, but it's a possibility. Adults in today's world have a lot of stress, perhaps more stress than ever before in the history of our country. We need to teach people how to deal with the stress so that their children don't suffer."

"It's confusing," Lexi admitted.

"I understand that, but it's very important for all of us to be aware that this goes on in our society. One of the common characteristics of child abusers is that they themselves were abused when they were young. They have learned wrong child-raising behavior."

"It's like passing a lesson down from one generation to the next?" Lexi remembered what her mother had said.

"Exactly," Mrs. Winston nodded. "It's a cycle that social workers and doctors want to break. It's certainly no excuse for anyone to abuse a child, but if that's the way you've been treated, you may not know any better."

"If this has been happening all along, why didn't Nicole tell anyone until just now?"

"It's very difficult for children to admit that they have been hurt by their very own parents. Children have a great deal of loyalty toward their parents."

"Besides," Todd added, "she was probably afraid that she'd be hurt again for telling on them."

Mrs. Winston nodded. "Oftentimes, an abused child doesn't feel she can trust anyone, Lexi. Nicole learned to trust Binky. That speaks very highly of the kind of person Binky is."

Binky, who'd been silent at the far end of the couch, finally gave a weak smile. "I guess it's really Nicole that matters, isn't it?" she said.

Impulsively, Lexi stood up and moved to where Binky was sitting. She threw her arms around her. "Binky, I want you to know I have been praying that you would do the right thing."

"Well, if I were you, I wouldn't worry about it

anymore," Mrs. Winston said.

"You are doing the right thing for Nicole and even for her father," Lexi affirmed.

Binky's expression was hopeful. "I want to believe that, Lexi. I really do."

Mrs. Winston stood up. "It's time for me to be going home. Do you kids want a ride? Or would you like to stay a little longer?"

"I'd better go too," Binky said. "My parents will be expecting me."

Lexi walked the threesome to the door. After they left, she stood staring out across the rolling lawn to the street, her eyes unfocused, her mind a million miles away. She was jarred out of her reverie when Ben came roaring down the stairs, making squealing sounds and waving his arms like the wings of the airplane.

"Vrrrrooom! Vrrrrooom! The fighter pilot's coming in for a landing. Vrrrrooom!" He crashed squarely into Lexi's back as she stood in the doorway. She staggered against the doorframe, catching herself.

"Whoa, Ben! What do you think you're doing?"

"Vrrrrooom! The fighter pilot just landed!" he said in a very loud voice.

"Benjamin Leighton, you're not supposed to knock people over," she scolded.

Ben's expression turned contrite and his eyes grew large. "Lexi's mad?" he wondered. The little downed fighter pilot suddenly looked so bewildered that Lexi burst out laughing and scooped him into her arms. She held him tightly until he began to squeal in protest. When their mother came to see what the commotion was about, Lexi flung one arm around Mrs. Leighton as well.

"What's wrong with Lexi?" Ben asked his mother. "She's squeezing people!"

Mrs. Leighton gave a breathless laugh as she stroked her daughter's silky hair. "I don't know, Ben, but I'm rather enjoying it. I haven't had a hug this big for many days."

"Here's a bigger hug," Ben challenged and flung himself toward his father as he entered the room.

Soon all four Leightons were entwined in one large giggling, hugging mass. Mr. Leighton finally extricated himself with the excuse that he needed to start the grill. Ben followed him, his arms outspread, still making vrrrroooming sounds as they moved through the house and into the backyard.

While Lexi's mother tossed a salad, Lexi went to her room. From where she stood at her window, she could hear her mother humming in the kitchen and her father and Ben discussing the merits of Ben's toy airplane. With a rush of gratitude, Lexi closed her eyes. "Thank you, Father. Thank you for a family that's well and whole and happy."

It's funny, Lexi mused as she went downstairs to rejoin her family, *sometimes it's difficult to appreciate the simple things in life until you realize what it's like for families who don't have them.*

All through supper the empty eyes of Nicole Marlini continued to haunt Lexi.

Chapter Twelve

"Are you going to be tinkering with this car forever?" Lexi wondered. She dangled her legs over one fender of Todd's old Ford coupe. "I told Binky we'd meet her at the Hamburger Shack fifteen minutes ago. She said she'd earned enough money in the past few weeks to buy us all a shake."

Todd's head popped out from beneath the hood. "Just about done. Why don't you call Binky and tell her we'll be a few minutes late?"

"Never mind." Todd and Lexi's heads swiveled toward the doorway.

"I sat at the Hamburger Shack for ten minutes and decided I might as well walk down here." Binky gave Todd a smile. "I know how you are when you get under the hood of a car."

Todd grinned sheepishly. "Sorry about that, Bink."

"It's okay," Binky shrugged. "I'm used to Egg, remember?" Binky moved toward the car. "It's pretty quiet around here today," she observed.

Todd nodded. "Mike didn't have any appointments so he told me to watch the place while he went to the bank and the post office. That's another reason we're late. He should be back soon."

Binky peered at the tangled web of hoses, wires and bolts under the car's hood. "I don't see how you can figure anything out in there. It all looks like a bunch of greasy glop to me."

Todd grinned. "Well, Binky, I guess we each have our own talents. Mine seems to be sorting out this greasy glop and making it run again."

Lexi remained silent as her two friends talked. She stiffened slightly as Todd brought up the one subject that Binky was very sensitive about these days.

"What's going on with the Marlinis, Bink? Are you still working for them?"

Binky's eyes clouded and her expression became somber. "At first the Marlinis told me they wouldn't need me anymore, but Mrs. Marlini did call last night and ask if I'd take Nicole to the library tomorrow."

"She did?" Lexi said, surprised. "Well, that's wonderful."

Binky nodded. "I've seen Nicole a few times in the past few weeks. She hasn't changed very much, but she seems a little more relaxed somehow. She told me her mommy and daddy were going to 'appointments' uptown twice a week."

"Do you suppose it's for counseling?" Todd wondered.

Binky nodded. "That's my guess. I'm surprised she said anything at all. Children can act as if there's nothing wrong in their lives when everything is caving in around them."

"You can act as if there's nothing wrong only for so long, though," Lexi pointed out, "before something starts to fall apart."

Binky nodded, her expression grim. "And I happened to be there when things started to crumble." She shuddered. "These have been the worst weeks in my entire life."

"Worst and best," Lexi reminded her friend.

Binky looked puzzled. "Why do you say that?"

"Didn't Harry Cramer come into your life about the same time?" Lexi said with an impish grin.

"Oh." A blush crept up Binky's neck to her cheeks. "Him."

Todd hooted from under the hood of the car. "*Oh, him.* Come on, Binky. We know better than that."

For the first time since she'd been in the shop, Binky gave a genuine all-out grin. "Well, I must admit, Harry *is* pretty good for my self-esteem."

"And your reputation with Minda Hannaford," Todd pointed out. "She thinks any girl who can attract a guy like Harry Cramer must not be too bad, after all."

"Big deal," Binky snorted. "Being on Minda Hannaford's approval list isn't my idea of an accomplishment."

Lexi chuckled. "I wouldn't know. I've never been on it."

"No," Binky agreed, "maybe not, but Minda looks at you differently. She respects you."

"Respects me?" Lexi said with a look of surprise. "Why do you say that?"

"Because you don't care what she thinks—you don't try to make her happy or impress her. You're just yourself. Minda has to respect someone she can't control."

Lexi smiled at her friend. "Gee, you're pretty good for *my* self-esteem."

"What's all this self-esteem talk today?" Todd asked as he pulled a rag from his back pocket to wipe his hands.

"It's your mom's fault, actually," Binky said.

"My mother?" Todd questioned, not sounding terribly surprised. "Now what's she been up to?"

"She's been great to me, Todd, ever since this thing with Nicole Marlini came up," Binky said. "I've been to her office several times, just to talk. She's been trying to explain to me why parents abuse their children."

Lexi slid off the fender of the car and came around to where Binky and Todd were standing.

"Your mom says that parents who have high self-esteem are parents who *like* themselves. They are more able to love their children than parents who don't like themselves. Parents with low self-esteem are frustrated and angry and often take it out on their children."

"I guess I always figured if you had a lot of self-esteem, you were kind of stuck up, conceited—proud of yourself," Todd admitted.

Binky shook her head emphatically. "No, that's not it at all. Your mother's made me understand that having good self-esteem just means that you feel good about yourself, that you like yourself. Having self-esteem means you're happy that you are who you are and that you wouldn't want to be anyone else. Your mom thinks that if Mr. Marlini learns to feel better about himself, and can learn to handle some of the stress he has, he can change too. Once he likes himself better, he'll be more apt to treat Nicole as he should."

"So you mean child abuse is preventable?" Todd asked. "That if people could be taught to like themselves, it wouldn't happen?"

"Maybe not in every case," Binky replied, "but in some."

Todd gave a little whistle. "That's a pretty scary idea, Binky. People who are always down on themselves will most likely take out their feelings on somebody else."

Binky nodded, "I know. Your mom's been really patient with me. She's answered lots of questions. I'm finally beginning to understand that some people under stress in other areas of their lives sometimes take it out on the people they love."

"Love one another as God has first loved you," Lexi quoted. Todd and Binky both turned to her in surprise. "What?"

"Love one another. That's what it's all about, isn't it? If we're careful to give everyone we know positive strokes and build their self-esteem, that will help them to love someone else. It's like the ripple effect you get when you throw a stone into a pond. One little act of loving can reach out and touch all kinds of people."

"I never thought of it like that, but I suppose you're right." Binky stared knowingly at Lexi. "You always do that, don't you?"

"Do what?" Lexi said in surprise.

"Learn something from the Bible that tells us

how we're supposed to be living."

Lexi grinned. "It's a habit, Binky. I thought you'd be used to it by now."

Binky gave a sheepish grin. "When I first met you, I wasn't sure I'd ever get used to that part of you, Lexi, but I'm beginning to believe you're right. The Bible *does* have something to say about everything that happens to us, even in our plain, ordinary, everyday lives."

It wasn't often that Binky brought up God or the Bible or even the fact of Lexi's faith. Perhaps Nicole's pain wasn't wasted after all. Perhaps lives would ultimately be changed. God could make that happen. For now, all Lexi could do was to continue to pray for the Marlinis and for Binky.

Lexi slipped one arm around Binky's waist and the other around Todd. "Come on, you two. My stomach tells me I'm starving. I think we need to go to the Hamburger Shack and refuel."

"Good idea," Binky nodded emphatically. "You know? I do believe my appetite is coming back," she said happily. "I must be feeling better."

"Well, my appetite never left," Todd grinned. "Let's go."

Laughing and talking, the three closed up the shop. As they walked down the street, Lexi glanced up at the sliver of a moon peeking through the deepening dusk. It was going to be a beautiful night in Cedar River.

———

In book #8, Lexi befriends Anna Marie Arnold. Something serious is happening to her. Anna is losing weight, but Lexi has a hunch it's not because of normal dieting. And Egg's interest in bodybuilding takes an ugly turn. He's looking into using steroids.

A Note From Judy

I'm glad you're reading *Cedar River Daydreams*!
I hope I've given you something to think about as
well as a story to entertain you. If you feel you have
any of the problems that Lexi and her friends experience, I encourage you to talk with your parents, a
pastor, or a trusted adult friend. There are many people who care about you!

Also, I enjoy hearing from my readers, so if you'd
like to write, my address is:

Judy Baer
Bethany House Publishers
6820 Auto Club Road
Minneapolis, MN 55438

Please include an addressed, stamped envelope if
you would like an answer. Thanks.